SCOTT MARIANI

HOUSE OF MALICE

CLAYMORE PUBLISHING

Published by Claymore Publishing

Copyright © Scott Mariani 2013

www.scottmariani.com

Scott Mariani asserts the moral right to be
identified as the author of this work.

First published by
Claymore Publishing in 2013.

A CIP Catalogue of this book is available
from the British Library

Paperback: 978-0-9569226-3-2
Mobi ISBN: 978-0-9569226-1-8
EPub ISBN: 978-0-9569226-2-5

Artwork design and layout by
Chandler Book Design
www.chandlerbookdesign.co.uk

Printed and distributed by
Createspace

ONE

IT WAS THURSDAY, another in a string of sunny afternoons that October and exactly one month since Mandy Freeman's whole life had changed.

She still couldn't believe her luck, and was in a daze as she drove up the narrow street in the quaint Cotswold village of Fairwood.

'This is it,' she said to Buster, who was perched on the passenger seat of her little blue Kia. Buster didn't reply, just lolled his tongue and panted. He was Mandy's Jack Russell terrier. Ten years old, he'd been her near-constant companion since her early twenties. Now he was about to share the biggest adventure of her life so far. He looked as excited as she felt.

Mandy parked the Kia on a double-yellow line outside the broad windows of the solicitors' offices. The sunshine was gleaming over the name 'Flowers & Duffy Ltd' that was painted white on the glass. 'Here we go. Back in a minute, boy,' she said, her heart skipping. She got out, slammed the car door and disappeared inside the building.

Gideon Flowers was there in person to greet her, a

1

small grey man wearing a bow tie and the crooked grin that was his best approximation of a warm smile. 'Welcome to Fairwood,' he said as he handed over the keys. 'I'm sure you'll be very happy in Summer Cottage.'

Mandy spent as little time as possible over pleasantries, not because she didn't want to chat to Mr Flowers but because she was so anxious to tear the half a mile beyond the village outskirts to her new home. Minutes later, she emerged triumphantly from the solicitors' office clutching the keys in her fist, dived back into the car and took off up Main Street in the direction of her new home, with a smile a mile wide and her long black hair loose in the breeze from the rolled-down car windows. Buster sat looking out, enjoying the ride and tail wagging non-stop.

'See this place, Buster?' she said happily as they drove out of the village and through the winding country lanes, hedgerows and trees zipping past. 'This is going to be our home from now on. All the rabbits in the world for you to chase. As for me, well, maybe now I'll be able to get on with my book.' She beamed irrepressibly at the thought, and felt like thumping the steering wheel for joy. Bye, bye, London. Bye-bye living cooped up in a box living next door to troglodytes and surrounded by dirt and noise.

God, it felt good to have escaped.

'And our only neighbour is a whole field away,' she said brightly. 'An eccentric old lady with a house full of cats. What do you say to that, Buster?' At least, that was what Mrs James in the wool shop had told her, a piece of information that had emerged from one of Mandy's first exploratory visits to the village just a matter of weeks ago.

Peace at last. It was too wonderful for words.

In truth, she knew it would be a while before her

excitement settled down enough to let her start writing again. But there was no doubt in her mind that coming to live in the former home of Ellen Grace was going to provide all the inspiration any writer could ever wish for.

Mandy had idolised Ellen Grace since the age of thirteen. She'd read her novels until the covers cracked and the pages fell out. By her twenties, when she'd decided to become an author herself, to one day aspire to Ellen's phenomenal bestselling success had been her dream. She'd modelled her whole style on Ellen's, studied every word she'd ever set to paper and analysed her plots, gleaning all she could about her heroine's storytelling technique.

And now, as amazing as it sounded, she was moving into the cottage that had been Ellen Grace's home when she'd penned her biggest bestseller of all, *One Night In December*. The epic historical romance was a personal favourite of Mandy's – and of the twenty or so million other fans who'd loyally devoured everything Ellen Grace had ever written.

Mandy could see from the Sat Nav that she was just quarter of a mile from her destination. As a lumbering tractor pulled out of a side road up ahead and forced her to slow, she felt a stab of impatience and then decided to call Victoria. She couldn't resist telling her the good news.

Her friend answered on the first ring as if she'd been waiting to pounce on the phone. 'Well?' she said, breathless with expectation.

'Got the keys!'

Victoria let out a shriek. 'Brilliant!'

'I'm on my way there right now.'

'Right *now*? Oh, my God…'

'I can't believe it's happening, Vic. No stopping me any more.'

'When do I see it?'

'Soon, I promise. It's just an empty house for now. Furniture's not coming until tomorrow morning.'

'I don't care, I want to see it!'

'Give me a little while to get settled in, then I'll email you some pics. You'll have to come and stay. You're going to love it.'

'I'm so pleased for you. This is just what you needed. You've had a rough year. Pretty soon you won't even remember James.'

'Who?' Mandy said, and they both laughed. 'Actually,' Mandy said. 'I think I might have met someone.'

'As in, a guy?'

'He lives in the village. His name's Todd. First time I came to view Summer Cottage, I found this café to have lunch. Busy little place, only one table free. I ended up sharing it with him. We got on really well. In fact, we got on great.'

'Tell me about him.'

'He's a photographer. Tall, dark, good looking, a year older than me—'

'And he's not married and not gay? Wow, what are the chances?'

'Divorced four years, no kids.'

'What was I telling you? It's like, fate, or something. This was all meant to happen. First Ellen Grace's old cottage falls into your lap at this amazing price. Now you meet the guy of your dreams.'

'Let's not get too carried away, Vic,' Mandy said with a smile. 'Anyway, I don't believe in fate. It's just luck, that's all. The house happened to be put on the market at the same time my divorce settlement was going through.

For once in my life things are coming together.'

'And you deserve it, babe.'

The tractor turned off. Summer Cottage was just up ahead. Mandy hurriedly said goodbye to her friend, promised to be in touch again soon and ended the call. Moments later, the property appeared through the trees.

'We're here,' she said to Buster.

TWO

MANDY SMILED EVEN more widely when she saw the name 'Summer Cottage' on the carved wooden plaque on the gate. *This is really happening*, she thought to herself.

Beyond the gate, a stone path wound its way between rose gardens on one side and a clipped lawn on the other, all the way up to the front steps of the house. Despite its diminutive-sounding name, it was quite a large, sprawling property: the only true, traditionally cottagey features it possessed were the thatched roof and the smallness of the leaded windows, many of which were charmingly surrounded with creeping ivy. Mandy couldn't wait to get inside and revisit the rambling interior.

She knew the place's history well. Built around 1682 and extensively restored from a near-ruin in modern times by its former owner, it was in stunning condition. What fortunes must have been lavished on it, she wondered for the hundredth time. And how simply incredible that she'd been able to afford the asking price, swapping a completely unremarkable one-bedroomed apartment in a featureless, increasingly run-down and crime-ridden suburb of

London for *this!* The divorce settlement from James had conveniently paid off the mortgage on the apartment just in time; at which point six years of deeply unhappy marriage, and the betrayal of his infidelity, had suddenly paid off by turning her into a woman of property and very soon afterwards the owner of what had to be one of England's most desirable period homes. Especially for her. The connection with the author Ellen Grace was an added bonus that Mandy was certain meant more to her than any other prospective buyer.

No, she definitely couldn't believe her luck.

She took out the ring of old-fashioned keys Gideon Flowers had given her, and offered one of the largest pair of them up to the front door lock, a massive black iron affair cast in the shape of a lion's head and held to the ancient oak door with flat-head rivets.

The lock turned. The heavy door swung open without a creak. Jittery with excitement, Mandy stepped through into the large entrance hall. Her footsteps rang off the stone floor tiles. The hall was empty apart from an antique dial telephone nestling in an alcove by the window. Buster trotted along in her wake, looking happy, even proud, as if he fully understood the importance of the moment.

The first thing Mandy noticed after she'd got her breath back was the bouquet of white roses that had been left for her, sitting in a pretty vase on the floor in a corner of the entrance hall. Going over to admire them, she saw there was a label attached to the neck of the vase, on which a note had been written. It was from Sarah, Ellen Grace's daughter and only child, from whom Mandy had bought the place.

White roses were mother's favourite, so it seemed
an appropriate way to welcome you. She'd
have been delighted that a fellow author should
take over Summer Cottage after she was gone.
Wishing you the very best of joy, health and
prosperity in your new home

– Sarah Grace

P.S. You have my mobile number, so don't
hesitate to call if you need anything. x

Mandy smiled sadly. The way people talked about Ellen Grace, even her own daughter, it was as if she was dead instead of …

Her thoughts were interrupted by the shrill and sudden jangling of the telephone in the hallway. She jumped at the sound, wondered who on earth could be calling – then remembered that she'd already given the number out to a few select people. She picked up the heavy receiver, but instead of a caller's voice there was a tone alerting her of a new message. It might be Chester Durham, her London-based literary agent, calling with news about the new book deal he was in the middle of brokering with her publishers. Not quite sure the old phone could handle such modern sophistication, she dialled 1-5-7-1 to find out.

The phone worked, but the message wasn't from Chester. Mandy sighed as she heard the familiar, pointed tone of voice.

'This is your mother. Remember me? I've been trying to call you all morning. I take it that you just don't want to pick up. I know you think it's wonderful and all that that you've got the

place you wanted. And you know I only want you to be happy. But I still think it's a folly, dear. A complete and absolute folly. I mean, what if it turns out you've been sold it on false pretences? This Grace woman might suddenly turn up, you know. There was never any proof that she was dead. Probably just gone wandering off – she was *a writer, after all, and everybody knows they're all stark staring mad. Not you, darling. Not yet, anyway. I know you've done not too badly out of it. Though I wish you'd get yourself a proper—'*

Mandy had heard enough. She deleted the message without listening to the rest of it and put down the receiver with a satisfied smile. 'Bye, Mother.' If only it were that easy to shut her up when you were face to face.

She turned to Buster, who was sitting in the middle of the hall watching her intently. 'Time for the grand tour,' she said.

The dog padded in Mandy's wake around the empty living room, where she paused to gaze lovingly at the carved oak fireplace; then into the large slate-floored country kitchen with its deep, square Belfast sink, fitted reproduction-antique cupboards and worktops and a door leading out to the back garden. But when she left the kitchen and turned left into the winding passage to explore the rest of the ground floor, he began to whine and seemed not to want to accompany her.

'What is it?' she asked him. 'Don't you want to see the rest of your new home?' Then, noticing the way he seemed to want to hang about the kitchen, she realised what was up. 'I get it. You're thirsty, aren't you? Hold on, I'll get you some water.' She trotted out to the car and brought in the plastic bag in which she'd packed a selection of doggy essentials, among them his water dish. She filled it from the tap in the kitchen and laid it down on the slate for him to slurp at. Leaving him to his devices, she shut the kitchen door and went on exploring the house.

It was even more wonderful than she remembered, with beamed passageways and twisting corridors leading here and there to studded oak doors and beautiful little rooms, each with its own unique and delightful period features. When she'd finished admiring the ground floor she ran up the wooden staircase to check out the upstairs. Of the cottage's three bedrooms, the one she'd already chosen for herself was an airy, secluded space at the end of a long, narrow passage. Mandy was certain that the bedroom, with its own tiny ensuite bathroom and a splendid view across the wildflower meadow to the rear of the cottage, had been Ellen Grace's choice before her. The passage leading to it was dark and windowless, lit only by a series of quaint old-fashioned wall lamps designed like lanterns, each with its own clunky Bakelite switch. It was a joy to walk up the passage, clicking lights on as you went, then swinging open the heavy arched door into the brilliant sunlit space of the bedroom. Mandy's heart thrilled at the idea that this was her very own.

Returning down the winding staircase, she found herself unable to resist the urge to go back into the room that was to be her writing study. The view from its twin windows was as beautiful as that from the bedroom: across the wavy fields, a line of beech trees were just beginning to turn golden.

This is it, she said to herself. *I'm here. I've arrived. This place will be good for me.*

And now it was time to begin the task of getting herself organised before the furniture arrived tomorrow.

Running back out to the car, she fetched her travel bag, dumped it in the hallway and unzipped it. Inside was her first-night survival gear: basic foodstuff, her rolled up sleeping bag and inflatable pillow, pyjamas, toilet bag and other assorted items.

She'd also packed something completely non-essential but which she'd wanted to be the very first object to decorate her new home. It was the framed August 2002 *Starstuck* magazine cover, featuring a photo of Ellen Grace outside Summer Cottage, that had hung above Mandy's writing desk in London; now it would take pride of place in her writing room here, having come back full circle to where the picture had been taken. It showed the famous author, with her trademark platinum-blond curls, beaming smile and the beautiful Victorian cameo pendant she always wore, posing in front of the cottage's entrance shortly after the refurbishment work on the building had been completed. Around that time, Ellen had started work on her novel, *One Night in December*.

Mandy carried the picture through to the writing study like a holy relic. There was a hook on the wall that was perfectly positioned to hang it between the twin windows overlooking the meadow, almost as if it had been put there on purpose.

She hung the picture up and stood back, shaking her head in wonder. 'This is weird,' she breathed aloud. Gazing at it, she could almost sense the presence of Ellen Grace in the house. It was so real, it was virtually tangible.

Her mother's words came back to her. *She might just turn up, you know. There was never any proof that she was dead.*

And Mandy wondered for a moment. Just for a moment. Might Ellen Grace ever return?

THREE

BECAUSE IN FACT, the events surrounding Ellen Grace's disappearance in November 2005 were still shrouded in mystery.

She had been born Georgina Ellen Potts fifty-two years earlier, the only daughter of Lyndon Potts, a bank clerk, and Judith, a history teacher, in the country town of Whitchurch, Shropshire. She could read fluently by the age of four, by seven was writing her own little stories, and by eight was developing full-sized novels imbued with the historical themes that were a passion she'd inherited from her mother. Just nine years later, she'd won a scholarship to Cambridge to read English Lit. It was there that she met and fell in love with a dashing young final-year medical student named Harry Grace. When Harry graduated and left Cambridge to work as a GP in the Peak District, to her parents' dismay Ellen, who'd now dropped the name Georgina, quit her studies and followed him.

Harry and Ellen were married at a little church in Buxton. Ellen found part-time work as a library assistant, which brought little extra money to the household but allowed her to indulge her passion for books. In the second year of the marriage, Ellen became pregnant; in the summer of 1973 Sarah, who would be their only child, was born.

The years passed. Ellen went on working at the library, eventually becoming its manager. In the meantime, she'd resumed her childhood pastime of writing historical fiction, now with a romantic twist. To begin with, she didn't regard her stories as anything more than for her own amusement. It was Harry who first suggested that she should submit one to a popular women's magazine. To Ellen's amazement, they not only accepted it right away for publication but offered payment and seemed keen to see anything else she'd written. She duly sent them a whole stack of short stories.

Over the next two years, they published every one of them. Ellen Grace the author was born. Inspired, she began writing in earnest and spent late nights working on the manuscript of what would become her first published novel, *A Maiden's Choice*. It was 1991.

It was during that phase of her life that tragedy tore the family apart.

Harry Grace was a conscientious and hard-working doctor who was devoted to his patients. When a misdiagnosed case of meningitis caused the avoidable death of a nine-year-old boy in his care, he took it badly and began to drink heavily.

The car was found smashed into a tree one wet night in October 1991. It took two hours for the fire crew to cut the vehicle open. Inside they found the corpse of its sole occupant, along with the bottle of vodka Dr Grace had apparently been clutching when the Saab had veered out of control and gone off the road at over fifty miles an hour. The autopsy showed him to be several times over the drink-drive limit.

Devastated, Ellen threw herself completely into her writing. *A Maiden's Choice* was published the following year. On the back of its instant runaway success, her publishers signed her to a six-figure four-book deal that made headlines in the trade press. *A Promise Made, A Promise Broken, Sir Radcliffe's Bride* and *The Black Rose* followed in quick succession and established their author as the leading light in British historical romantic fiction. She was hailed variously as 'the new Jane Austen', 'the new Charlotte Brontë' and 'the slush queen', depending on which critics you read. Ellen didn't heed the bad reviews. Her publishers and her agent loved her. Her bank manager loved her even more – as did the legions of devoted fans. Ellen adored her fans every bit as much in return. She gave generously of herself, answering every letter personally and always happy to give interviews. In private, her relationship with her daughter Sarah was less rosy. By now Sarah was twenty-seven and working internationally for an aid charity. They seldom saw one another.

It was in the spring of the year 2000 that Ellen, while travelling around the Cotswolds to research her next book, came across a badly neglected, virtually derelict seven-teenth-century cottage outside the village of Fairwood. It was a sinkhole for money, but by this stage in her writing career Ellen had all the money she needed, and more. She bought the cottage the same day she saw it, sold up the house in Buxton and moved to a rented manor on the other side of Fairwood while Summer Cottage was being restored to its former glory.

In June 2002, the restoration was complete. During the two years the project had taken, in between overseeing its progress Ellen had gone on working assiduously in her temporary home to produce *Take My Heart* and *Julia's Tale*. The combined advance fees she earned for both bestsellers just about covered the vast cost of turning Summer Cottage from a semi-derelict shell surrounded by a miserable weed-bound acre to a magnificent period home standing in one of the prettiest landscaped gardens in the county.

It was that August that the photo had been taken and made it to the cover of *Starstruck* magazine, one of the leading celeb glossies. The image stuck. For millions of her fanatical readers, Ellen Grace and Summer Cottage became synonymous, entwined in literary legend.

Though in fact, as some critics had unpopularly pointed out since those days, Ellen Grace had already passed her peak as an author by the time she came to live there. She wrote only one more novel during her days at Summer Cottage. *One Night in December* was her biggest bestseller, if not her greatest critical success.

After its publication, instead of launching straight into the next book as her fans had become used to her doing, Ellen Grace went silent. There were no more novels. No more replies to fan mail. No more interviews. Photographers would occasionally try to get a snap of her at Summer Cottage, whose curtains remained drawn for weeks on end. The last known photo had been taken by a fan who'd virtually had to camp in the grounds to get a glimpse of her. It showed a thin, wasted, ashen-faced woman peeking furtively, almost fearfully, through a gap in the curtains. The radiant, smiling Ellen Grace the world had known seemed to have withered away.

Rumours weren't slow to spread. The word was that Ellen Grace had 'gone strange'. Why the sudden reclusion? Was she ill? Depressed? Many questions were asked. No answers ever came to light.

One misty day in late November 2005, a rare visitor appeared on the doorstep of Summer Cottage. Burt Barrington of the Barrington & Liddle Literary Agency in Kensington had tried and failed for almost a month to get his client on the phone. Under pressure from Ellen's publishers to get her signature on a hot new contract that would reinvigorate her career and sales, he'd driven down from London in person to see her.

Barrington would later describe his shock at finding the front door hanging open. He told reporters how he'd knocked and called her name repeatedly before venturing inside.

Ellen Grace was not there. She had disappeared.

Nobody ever saw her again.

FOUR

AFTER ROUGHING IT for her first night in Summer Cottage, Mandy was happy to see the removals lorry roll up outside right on schedule the following morning.

Suddenly, the serene atmosphere of the empty house was filled with noise and bustle as the men tramped back and forth carrying crates, boxes and furniture through the hallway and into the various rooms. Mandy was in the middle of the activity, directing them here and there and supplying them with tea and biscuits. Her old upright piano went into the dining room, against the wall nearest the biggest window where it would get the light. Her desk and bookcase went into the writing study. The trickiest part was getting her wardrobe and bed up the tight stairway, but after a lot of heaving and sweating they were finally in place without any damage having been done.

As the last of the load was brought in, Mandy began to realise how little stuff she actually possessed. What had filled her tiny place in London to bursting point scarcely seemed to take up any room here. It looked as if a series of major antiques centre shopping sprees were going to be in order. 'Have to start selling more books, Buster,' she said to the dog. 'Maybe one day, we'll have as many bestsellers as Ellen did. What do you say to that?'

The Jack Russell looked up at her with mournful eyes, and not for the first time since yesterday she wondered what was wrong with him. Normally a happy, playful sort of dog, he'd been restless and whingeing all yesterday evening, and this morning had been moping about with his tail between his legs looking decidedly morose. She hoped he was all right. Ten wasn't that old for a Jack Russell. Most likely, it was the disruptive presence of the removal men bothering him, on top of the general stress of moving house. She'd read that dogs could be very affected by it. Or was it cats? She couldn't remember now.

Thinking that the vase of white roses Sarah Grace had kindly left her would look nice on the window-sill of her new writing study, she went into the entrance hall to retrieve it. 'Damn,' she said when she saw the state the roses were in, badly wilted and shrivelled. The water in which the stems stood had turned a murky shade of slimy green. 'Should have put them in the light,' she scolded herself. There was nothing for it but to chuck them away.

Afterwards, she returned to the task of unpacking. First things first: her several large boxes of books. It seemed only fitting that Ellen Grace's titles should be the first to be put up on the bookcase. Mandy arranged them, left to right, in chronological order of publication, the way she'd always done: from *A Maiden's Choice* to her much-prized signed hardback copy of *One Night in December*, a book she'd queued for four hours to have autographed by the author on the one magical, all-too-brief occasion Mandy had come face to face with her idol.

And there it now stood on the shelf, in the very place that Ellen had penned that final novel.

She was busily unpacking clothes in the bedroom a little while later when she heard the ringing of the old-fashioned telephone and hurried downstairs to answer it. 'Hello?'

'What happened to your mobile? I've been calling and calling.'

That was Chester's way. Evidently, literary agents were just too busy and efficient to bother with minor details like "Hi, Mandy, how are you? Hope you're getting settled in all right".

'Trouble getting reception in the house,' she said. 'I think it's the thick walls.'

'I hope your skin's as thick as your walls are,' he said. Another of Chester's little habits. He didn't waste time on chit-chat.

Mandy tensed. This was the news about her new book deal that she'd been anticipating, and so far it didn't sound good. 'Go on, let's have it,' she said.

'I just had a long talk with Katie Piggott.'

'And what does my illustrious editor have to say for herself? I suppose they won't increase their advance offer from the last contract?'

A pause. 'It's worse than that, Mandy. I'm afraid they don't want any more books from you at all. Before you say anything, it's not just you. They're not renewing contracts with *any* of their historical romance authors.'

'Jesus.' She hadn't expected great news, but this was a shock.

'I really tried. But it's no go. Not unless you're willing to take a whole new direction.'

'What kind of whole new direction?' Mandy asked stiffly.

'Erotica's the thing now. Everyone's getting on board with it.'

'You mean jumping on the bandwagon just because some publisher in the USA managed to sell a boatload of it.'

'Call it what you want.'

'Come on, Chester. I can't write that stuff. It's just glorified porn.'

'Sure it is. Who cares? That's what selling out there right now. It's your only option if you want to cut a new deal with them.'

'They're not the only publishers, are they? What about Orion, have you approached them? Or Random House?'

Chester heaved a sigh. 'Mandy, I'd already done the rounds before I even spoke to Katie. I hate to tell you, but the fact is nobody's going to want *Lady Cordelia's Secret*. Maybe if the last book's sales had been a little stronger …'

'Maybe if Miss Piggy had tried promoting it better—'

'Yeah well, that's in the past now. Let's deal with the present reality. As your agent I can only advise you to sit down and try to come up with something different.'

'I can make *Lady Cordelia* different.'

'Forget Lady Cordelia, okay? I mean something totally new.'

'I've been working flat out on that for seven months.'

'Put it down to experience.'

'Just like that,' she said bitterly.

'And maybe a change of name wouldn't hurt, either.'

'What am I, publishing poison?'

Mandy could hear another of the agency office phones ringing in the background. 'Listen,' Chester said, 'I've got to rush. Mull over what I've said. And have a think about what pseudonym you could go out under. Why *not* have a go at writing erotica? Act like a pro. You are a published author, after all. Okay? Talk soon.'

And he hung up and left her standing there, staring helplessly around her at this house she'd just bought.

Two hours later, the fledgling and as yet nameless writer of erotica was sitting at her desk having a very bad time thrashing out her opening chapter. It hadn't taken long to come up with a storyline, some generic and perfectly commercial fluff about a reporter named Desi who became entangled, both professionally and literally, with a handsome racing driver. That was the easy part. The hard part was laying down the bad prose that came with the territory. It just wouldn't flow. Mandy had never, ever rehashed and rewritten a paragraph as often as:

> His face was lean and hard, his thick shock of sun-bleached blond hair set off by the deep tan of a man who spends most of his time in exotic locations. A thin smile played on his lips, lips that were somehow both sensual and cruel. As he stepped towards her he reached up with a slim, strong hand and took off his designer sunglasses to reveal a penetrating blue gaze. His eyes were sharp, hawk-like, narrowed by the sun. They darted up and down the length of Desi's body, and it almost felt to her as though hands were running across her bare skin. He seemed to like what he was seeing.

'Shit, I can't write this crap! It's sub-mental!' Mandy highlighted the entire text and stabbed the Delete key with such venom that the laptop screen wobbled on its hinges. Glaring at the now-blank screen and realising that she'd just totally wasted the last two hours, she let out a yell of frustration and banged on the desk with the flat of both hands.

As if shaken from its mounting, the framed picture of Ellen Grace dropped off the wall and landed on the floor with a thud.

'Oh no!' Mandy cried out. The frame was nothing special, but the picture itself was irreplaceable. She rushed over to pick it up, and anxiously checked it over. Thankfully, it appeared undamaged. She hung it back on its hook.

'Thanks a bloody million, Chester. This is all your fault,' she muttered ungraciously.

She couldn't bear to go back to the computer. She paced the room instead, feverishly racking her brain. There must be something else she could do, she thought. Maybe a rom-com – they were always popular. Or how about a detective story? If Chester wanted a new image for her, why not reinvent herself as a crime author? She could write a whole series, even write it under a male pseudonym. Wouldn't be the first writer to do so. Chester would love it … But no, no, crime was too complicated. Too much nitty-gritty research to do. You had to write what you were passionate about, and rom-com was more Mandy's style. She decided that Chester could whistle for his crime series.

Coffee suddenly seemed like a wonderful idea. Mandy trotted into the kitchen. Buster was coiled up in his bed, peering up at her with that worried look he had when he'd done something wrong. Near the back door was a small pool of what was unmistakably urine.

'Oh, Buster,' she groaned. She knew it was both pointless and cruel to shout at him. As she cleared up the mess, she said in a gentle tone, 'You could have let me know you needed to go outside, no? You're not a pup any more. What's got into you?' And it *was* unusual. Buster could go for ever without peeing, and had been completely housetrained since he'd been tiny. She knelt down beside him and patted his small, hard head. 'I'm sorry, pet, did I stress you out with all that banging and shouting earlier? I wasn't yelling at you. I was yelling at … oh, never mind.' Why burden the poor thing with her human problems? Dogs didn't know how lucky they were.

Buster skulked out of bed, crept to the back door and stood there looking entreatingly back at her. Mandy opened the door and let him out into the garden. He seemed happy, even relieved, to get out of the house. Instantly, his whole body language was different, tail wagging high. Two wood pigeons were strutting about the lawn; Buster spotted them and gave chase with an excited bark.

After she'd finished mopping up the last of the mess, Mandy washed her hands and made herself a coffee. She savoured a few gulps of the warm drink and then headed back to the study, cup in hand, to check her emails. Who knows, she thought, a publisher might have had a last-minute change of heart about *Lady Cordelia*.

She walked into the study and stopped dead. She almost dropped her cup.

The picture of Ellen Grace had fallen off the wall again. Except this time, it was lying several feet away from the skirting board, well out towards the middle of the room.

'I don't believe this!' She ran over and picked it up. This time the precious picture *was* damaged, damn it. One lower corner of the glass was cracked where it had landed badly. Part of the pane was missing and there were shards on the floor. Worse, there was a laceration on the picture itself where a sharp edge had gashed it. 'Oh, shit,' she muttered.

She frowned. How had it come to be lying where it was, so far away from the wall? It almost looked as if it had been thrown there. Had Buster moved it? Impossible, Buster was still outside in the garden, and before that he'd been closed in the kitchen. Maybe the picture had somehow bounced towards the middle of the room on hitting the floor, but that seemed weird.

That was when Mandy noticed that it wasn't just the picture that had fallen. Three books were lying on the floor where they'd somehow managed to slide off the shelf. She laid the cracked picture and her cup on the desk, went over to pick them up and saw that all three were Ellen Grace books: her well-thumbed paperback editions of *Take My Heart* and *Julia's Tale* and the signed hardback of *One Night in December*. None of the other books appeared disturbed.

Completely baffled as to how they could have fallen, she carefully replaced them on the shelf, lining them up neatly as she always did. She was virtually nerdy when it came to caring for her books, not like some writers she knew who stacked them in teetering piles all over the place. Which made it all the less likely that they'd just topple off her shelf like that.

Perplexed, Mandy grabbed a waste paper basket and went back over to where the picture had fallen, to pick up the little shards of glass on the floor. She was just about to kneel down when she heard a sound.

She froze, tensed.

That wasn't Buster, either.

The sound was right behind her in the room.

She jumped to her feet, whirled round to face the study door and let out a cry of fright.

The figure of a woman in black stood in the doorway. Staring at her.

FIVE

'WHO ARE YOU?' The woman asked, still staring at Mandy from the study doorway. She was tall and upright, with white-streaked silver hair swept away from her forehead. Her face was long and chalky-white, her expression cold and severe. There was a peculiar glimmer in her eyes that Mandy found extremely disconcerting.

For a moment, her heart pounding, Mandy was speechless; then, recovering from the shock, she replied hotly, 'I might ask you the same question. This is my house you're in.'

The old woman's stony face didn't flicker. 'Dinky Dora is missing. I don't suppose you've seen her?'

Mandy now realized who the woman was: Mrs Bannister, her nearest neighbour. She was nothing like the charming little old eccentric lady she'd imagined and had been looking forward to meeting. 'No, I'm afraid I haven't seen Dinky Dora,' Mandy said, making no effort to hide her annoyance. 'I don't even know who Dinky Dora is. I suppose she's one of your cats?'

'Dinky Dora is terrified of dogs.'

'Listen, Mrs Bannister – that is your name, isn't it? I've got work to do. I hope you find your cat.'

'She's black, you know. With a white tip on her tail.'

'I'll be sure to keep an eye out for her,' Mandy said, trying to speak in a softer tone as she guided Mrs Bannister back out of the study doorway and towards the entrance hall. 'Don't worry about my dog – he wouldn't hurt a fly. And next time you decide to pay me a visit, would you mind knocking before you come in? You really gave me a fright.'

There was an awkward silence during which the old woman stood and gazed around her with a dreamy, faraway look. 'Seems strange,' she murmured.

'What seems strange?' Mandy asked, wanting this interruption to be over and the woman out of her house.

'This place, without Ellen in it. She loved Summer Cottage. She'd never have left it willingly.'

'No?'

'Oh, no. That's what I told the police but they wouldn't listen. Nobody would listen to me. That daughter of hers had no right to sell it. She's a piece of w—'

'Yes, well, she did sell it. It belongs to me now, okay? By the way, I'm Mandy. Mandy Freeman.'

The woman didn't reply. She stood there staring archly at Mandy for a few seconds, then she turned on her heel towards the entrance hall.

Mandy wondered how well Ellen Grace and her neighbour had known each other. Had they been close friends? There were so many questions she wanted to ask, but the woman's strangeness made her hold back. What a pity – and how typical that the first person she'd met who happened to know Ellen Grace personally turned out to be an oddball.

After the unexpected neighbourly visit, Mandy's concentration was too broken to go on struggling to get anything written that day. The afternoon seemed to have passed by quickly; it was already getting dark outside as the days moved deeper into autumn. She mooched around aimlessly for a while, then thought about calling Todd, the guy she'd met in the village. She found his photographer's business card in her purse and dialled his number, wondering if it was too forward to invite him over for a meal.

Todd seemed delighted to hear from her. 'Mandy! I was wondering when we'd bump into each other again. No, I'm not doing anything tonight – I'd love to come over.'

'Don't expect too much, though,' she warned him. 'I don't have much of a larder yet. It won't be anything fancier than scrambled eggs on toast.'

'Don't you worry about that. I think I can rustle us up something. The village deli won't be closing for another twenty minutes. If you like, I could pick up a few things and bring them over later.'

'Are you sure?'

'Sure I'm sure. See you soon.'

Mandy spent the next hour unpacking the last of what little crockery and cutlery she had, and putting the kitchen in order. Soon afterwards, there was a rap at the door and she trotted to the entrance hall to find Todd standing there clutching a large bag of groceries and a bottle of champagne, which he thrust at her as he stepped inside. 'House warming present,' he said. 'It's great to see you again, Mandy.'

The same easy rapport still existed between them as when they'd first met. It was as if they'd known each other for years. She felt comfortable in his presence, and strongly attracted. She hoped he felt the same frisson she was feeling.

'You shouldn't have!' she said, looking in amazement at the champagne.

'We're celebrating your arrival in Fairwood, aren't we? Stick it in the freezer and it'll be chilled in time for dinner.' He rustled the grocery bag. A long packet of spaghetti protruded from the top. 'You like Italian?'

'Spaghetti with champagne?'

'Are you kidding? Champagne'll go with anything. Now lead me to your kitchen and let your chef for the night get to work. I even brought a few utensils in case you didn't have them.'

'How pathetic of me,' she said as they headed into the kitchen. 'First I invite you for a meal, then I let you do the cooking. I won't even be able to help much, either. I'm not exactly Delia Smith.'

He emptied the groceries and cooking utensils out on the pine table and grinned at her. 'You don't have to do a thing. I'm delighted to cook, though on one condition only. You've got to give me something in return.'

She cocked her head to one side, raising one eyebrow and looking at him with mock suspicion. 'Oh yeah? What's that?'

'The guided tour. I haven't seen round the place yet.'

'Deal,' she said.

They began with the downstairs. 'And this is where I'll be doing my writing,' she said as she showed him inside the study.

'Wish I had a space like this to work in,' he said, gazing around him and nodding. Noticing the broken picture lying on the desk, he pointed. 'Whoops. Had an accident?'

'That's a little odd, actually,' she replied, frowning at the picture. 'It keeps dropping off the wall.'

'Is this where it was hanging?' he asked, going over to examine the bare hook between the windows. He waggled it. 'No wonder. It's loose. How about letting the handyman bodge it for you?'

'Handyman, chef. Is there anything you can't do?'

'Truth? I'm not that much of a photographer.'

'I don't believe a word of it. Hey, if you could find a way of making the books stay on the shelves, too, that'd be great. They fell off earlier, which is a mystery to me.'

He shrugged. 'Could be trucks.'

'Trucks?'

'Moore's Haulage in Stanton. Their drivers often take a short cut down the country lanes around Fairwood. Some of those trucks are really massive, too big and heavy for these roads. There was an article in the Village Voice complaining about vibrations.'

'Maybe,' she said doubtfully.

'Don't worry about it,' he said with a bright smile. 'I'll gladly take a look at the bookshelf for you sometime. Why don't you show me around the rest of the place, and then we'll eat?'

The living room was next. 'I love it,' Todd commented. 'Whoever restored the place did a really sympathetic job. Look at all these period features, the beams, and all these nooks and crannies everywhere. And the fireplace. Wow. What an amazing piece of carving.' She followed as he walked across the gleaming floorboards for a closer look at the massive piece of oak. Below the thick mantel jutted a fierce animal head, gargoyle-like, its features still sharply drawn even after centuries. The effect was strikingly Gothic.

'I wondered what it represents,' she said. 'A lion, like the one on the front door?'

'Or a griffin, maybe,' he said, running his fingers over the smooth, glistening wood. 'Some heraldic beast of Olde England. What a fabulous piece of historic workmanship to have in your home.'

'It's so rambling, you could lose yourself in it,' Todd marvelled as she showed him more of the downstairs, proudly pointing out her favourite features.

She laughed. 'I keep thinking there are still more rooms for me to discover.'

'What's along that passage?' he asked when she'd led him upstairs.

'My bedroom,' she replied, hoping that didn't sound like an invitation.

'I love these old light fittings,' he said, tapping one of the old Bakelite switches in the passage. He turned it on and off with a solid click. 'They don't make stuff like that any more. And the old-fashioned heavy oak doors with metal studs in them, and the ironware, like the ring handles and the big old keys in every lock. Very cool.'

'So the overall verdict?' she said, smiling broadly at him over her shoulder as they made their way back downstairs. 'You approve?'

'It's marvellous. Apart from anything else, it's a photographer's dream.'

'Or will be, when it's properly furnished. That might have to wait until I get a bestseller or two.'

'You won't have to wait long, I'm sure.' Wandering back in for another admiring look at the dining room, he went over to the piano.

'Needs tuning,' she said as he lifted the lid.

He casually tinkled a few notes with his right hand. 'You play?'

She laughed. 'To hear me, you'd never think I'd started at age seven. You sound like you can find your way around a piano yourself, though.'

'It's not my forte.'

'Ouch. With puns like that you could go a long way in the publishing business.' She smiled at him. 'So you don't rate yourself much as a photographer, and you can't play the piano. Tell me, Todd Talby. There must be something you're best at.'

'In all the world?'

'In all the world.'

'I have a few regrets in life,' he said, thoughtfully tinkling a few more notes on the piano. 'One of them is that I never became a professional cook.'

'Really?'

'Don't get me wrong. I enjoy my job. I get to travel around a lot, I'm my own boss, I meet interesting people. But cooking's what makes me happy. I love to be around food. Thank Christ I don't love eating it as much as I love preparing it, or I'd be as fat as a fool.' He turned away from the piano. 'And speaking of food, now that you've met your end of the bargain by showing me your amazing house, it's time for me to fulfil mine. Let's get this meal on the road.'

With just a pack of spaghetti, a tin of peeled Italian tomatoes, some black olives and a wedge of parmesan cheese, a little olive oil, butter, garlic, basil, sea salt and ground pepper and just a touch of cream for the sauce, Todd expertly whipped them up a fabulous feast. By the time the food was heaped steaming on their plates, the champagne was nicely chilled. They sat across from one another at the pine table with Buster watching over them.

'Here's to Summer Cottage,' Todd said, raising his glass. 'Or should I say, here's to its very lucky and talented new owner.'

Mandy felt herself blush. 'And thank you for being here to share my first real meal in the place.'

The food tasted as delicious as it looked and smelled. As they ate and drank and laughed, Mandy was thinking she'd really like to spend more time with Todd. A lot more time.

'You talked about regrets,' she said.

'I have my fair share,' he admitted.

'Like what? Or is it too personal?'

'Like not having met someone like you years ago,' he said, looking very earnestly into her eyes.

She blushed again, and lowered her gaze. 'I'm glad I came here,' she said quietly. 'And not just because of the house.'

There was a silence between them. Then, perhaps sensing that the conversation was getting a little intense, Todd changed the subject. 'Met the neighbours yet?'

'Just the one,' she said, pulling a face.

Todd chuckled as she told him the story of Mrs Bannister's visit that afternoon. 'Have you seen Dinky Dora?' she said, affecting a creepy voice. 'That's her cat,' she explained. 'By the sounds of things her place is crawling with them.'

'I've heard she's a bit of a character,' Todd said. 'Keeps herself to herself. I've never seen her, even though I've lived in Fairwood for four years now.'

'If you ask me, she's more than a little weird. Gave me the creeps. Mrs Danvers came to mind.'

'Who the hell is Mrs Danvers?' he said, laughing.

'You know – from *Rebecca*. The nasty housekeeper?'

'I remember. Saw the old Hitchcock movie based on the book.'

'In Daphne du Maurier's novel she had a skull face, high cheekbones, sunken eyes, a lot scarier than the film. That's all I could think of when she suddenly appeared like that.'

'You writers.'

'I'm not kidding, Todd. She scared me shitless. Then started going on about Ellen not ever leaving this place willingly.' Mandy shook her head. 'I don't know why, but it got to me. I wish she hadn't come here.'

'Ah, yes,' he said. 'The mystery of the vanishing author.'

'Don't joke about it.'

Todd could see she really was affected by what had happened. 'I wouldn't worry about her, Mandy,' he said reassuringly. 'You know, there are cat people and there are dog people. I find that cat people are often a bit, well, *peculiar*. Take my sister Emma – she's got five of the things, and she's a right one. Dog people are much more normal. Aren't they, little fella?' he added, leaning down to pat Buster on the head. 'Especially Jack Russell owners.'

Buster growled. Todd drew his hand away quickly. 'Whoa.'

'I'm so sorry,' Mandy said, startled. 'He's never done that before.'

'It's okay. My fault.'

'He's been acting a bit strange since the move. Needs some time to settle in, I suppose.'

'Maybe Mrs Danvers put a spell on him,' Todd said.

'Thanks a million. That's what I really wanted to hear. How'd you feel if your nearest neighbour was a scary old witch or something?'

He reached across the table to gently touch her hand. 'Come on, Mandy. Lighten up. She's just winding you up, trying to freak you out. Don't take what she said seriously, okay? Ellen Grace is gone. Do you really think her daughter would have sold Summer Cottage to you if she thought her mum was going to turn up on your doorstep? That's just nuts.' He paused, looked out the window and drew a breath. 'My God!'

'What is it? Todd?' Mandy asked, alarmed.

'I've think I've just seen Mrs Danvers flying off on her broomstick, with a moggy on her shoulder.'

'Bastard.'

He grinned. 'Couldn't resist. Here, have some more champagne.'

By the time dinner was over, Mandy had forgotten all about her encounter with her neighbour. The two of them talked and laughed for a long time afterwards, and even Buster seemed in a happier mood. Finally, the time came for Todd to leave. It was an awkward parting. Both of them knew they were standing on the brink of a potentially serious relationship; neither of them wanted to appear either too forward or too noncommittal at this delicate stage. They managed a peck on the cheek, then with a wave Todd walked to his red Volvo estate and drove off into the night. She watched his taillights disappear down the road and shut the door, smiling to herself.

She was thinking about him as she got ready for bed, a warm glow spreading inside her from the champagne and the feeling that something deeper might develop between them. She wondered if he was having the same thoughts at home in his little terraced house in Fairwood. There was no question that they'd meet again very soon.

Once tucked up in bed, she tried to lose herself in a chapter from the Ellen Grace novel she was re-reading for the umpteenth time, but the champagne had made her drowsy. She laid the book down, switched off the bedside light and fell into a deep sleep.

SIX

MANDY AWOKE SUDDENLY, gripped by cold and shivering. Outside the cottage the wind was howling.

Thump ... thump. It was something moving behind the drapes that had woken her. She sat up in bed, momentarily startled before she realised that it was her bedroom window banging in the wind. She couldn't recall having left it open – mustn't have done up the latch properly, she supposed.

She reached out and switched on the bedside light, but it didn't come on. Had the bulb gone? Was there a power cut? In the darkness she clambered out of bed, gritting her teeth against the chill air, and began to make her way towards the window to close it.

In just a few steps, she found herself completely disorientated. The room seemed pitch black and she could no longer sense where the bed was, or in which direction to find the window. She stumbled blindly a few more steps until she felt the cold wall with her hand, and used it to guide her until she came to another wall.

She turned, reached out her arms and found that yet another wall was blocking her way. Suddenly the pitch-black space seemed to be closing in on her, so that her quickening breath sounded confined in a tightening trap.

The sweat breaking out on her brow turned chill as she heard what sounded like a low moan coming from inside the room. She wasn't alone in the darkness.

The walls were closing in even more, trapping her in here with some faceless presence that she could sense reaching out from the black shadows to touch her. She let out a ragged cry of terror and began to beat her fists against the clammy wall that blocked her escape. The window was banging wildly in the wind, which was roaring into the room and swirling violently all around her like a hurricane. The sound filled her head. She clapped her hands over her ears. Her scream was lost in the shriek of the gale.

And then the thing in the room was right beside her, raking her flesh as it clasped her in a bony embrace. A dread voice whispering meaningless horrors inside her head. She could smell the thing's corrupt breath, feel its disease touching her ...

Mandy awoke for real and sat up in bed with a shudder.

The bedroom was perfectly quiet. Not a breath of wind outside. Moonlight shone through the closed window.

It had been the most vivid nightmare she'd known in her life, and it took a few moments to persuade her that she was now fully awake. The bedclothes were tousled. Turning on the bedside light she peered anxiously around the room and then got up, feeling shaken and groggy. The alarm clock read 03:52. There was no way she'd get back to sleep easily after such a dream.

She padded barefoot downstairs to the kitchen, where she made herself a cup of cocoa. 'Can't you sleep either, Buster?' she said as he came sidling up to her. 'Looks like we both have a case of the nerves.' He followed her to the living room and hopped up on the sofa next to her. Mandy drank the reassuring cocoa in small sips until the mug was empty. Then she curled up on the sofa and lay cuddling Buster until, eventually, she fell asleep with the light on.

No more nightmares haunted her. When she awoke again, the morning sun was filtering through the living room curtains. Buster was already awake, sitting close by and watching her as she got up. Far from feeling stiff and tired after having slept on her old sofa, she felt strangely energized. An idea for a story had come to her waking mind. It wasn't fully formed, seeming to float nebulously around inside the part of her creative imagination that wasn't fully conscious. Experience had taught her not to chase it, or it would run like a startled deer and the precious inspiration would be gone. She had to relax her mind, not think about it too much, and let it come to her.

After a quick breakfast and seeing to the dog, she went straight to her writing room without even bothering to change out of her pyjamas. The idea in her mind now somehow felt ready to emerge into the light. She sat down at the desk, flipped open the laptop, quickly created a new blank document for herself. 'Okay,' she said. 'Here we go.' She closed her eyes, took a deep breath and began.

But as the ideas in her mind crystallised into words, something strange happened.

Something strange, and deeply disturbing. Within moments, she realised with a shock that what was coming out of her head, flowing out of her fingers and appearing on the screen in front of her, wasn't like anything she'd ever written before.

It was a horror story. And it was streaming out of her with a momentum she'd never experienced.

She stopped typing. Stared at what she'd written. 'What the—?'

Where had these words come from? She'd no idea. But there they were, black on white on the screen in front of her, undeniably the product of her own mind. She couldn't stop herself. Her fingers seemed to return to the keys of their own will, and the stream of words continued.

After almost four years as a professional fiction author, Mandy had no illusions about her skill at the craft. Her ability with the instrument that was her writer's voice was that of a competent technician, no more. She could tell a story, and tell it adequately to suit the relatively simple needs of the readership she was familiar with – but she was no wizard, still less a virtuoso with words. There was always a lot of pencil-chewing involved, lots of coffee breaks for soul-searching and "inspiration". It generally didn't come that easily to her.

But now, suddenly, everything was different. The words were pouring out of her faster than she could type, her fingers a flurry on the clicking keys. She felt fully in command, effortlessly capable of summoning up ideas and images with a clarity, a vividness that was stunning, even alarming. It was as though the words were coming from some other source, and she was just channelling them, objectively, like a medium.

Her fingers clicked faster and faster. Line after line filled the screen, page after page. Lost a whirlwind of words, she sat there in growing awe and simply *watched* the writing appear.

What was happening to her?

'No!' she said out loud. This had to stop. It took an effort to tear her hands from the keys. She pulled away from the desk, stood up and edged away from the desk.

But something was dragging her back, and her will wasn't strong enough to resist the call. She returned to the desk. Her hands were drawn once more to the keys. Her fingers began to move, like puppet fingers suspended on invisible threads and operated by an unseen force.

And on it came, relentlessly. A macabre outpouring that terrified her as much as it gripped her. The air around her seemed to thicken. Her peripheral vision melted away into a black-red haze so that all that existed was the screen, a living, pulsating thing filling her world.

It was the sound of Buster barking in the kitchen that abruptly jerked her back to reality. She broke away from the screen, snatched her fingers from the keys with a gasp. Their tips were red and tender. She looked at the clock on her desk and couldn't believe it. It was nearly 1 p.m. She'd been writing non-stop for the last five hours. The word count in the bottom corner of her screen stood at 8,503.

Unbelievable. She'd started with a completely blank document. Her morning's output was more than five times what she could produce on a normal working day, and a good one at that.

But when she began to read back what she'd written, she felt sick. It was horrifying to think these images and ideas had come out of her head. Just as she'd done with her failed attempt at erotica, she highlighted the whole eight and a half thousand words and deleted them. To be rid of them properly and completely she clicked into her computer's recycle bin. *Are you sure you want to permanently delete this file?* the computer prompted her.

'You bet I do,' she said. And the file was gone, flushed down the toilet where it belonged.

Buster was still barking. What was the matter with him? Then Mandy realised why: there was someone at the front door. She got up from the desk and went to see who it was.

When she wrenched the door open, the broad shape of Chester Durham was standing there grinning toothily at her. He was wearing the same dark business suit he always wore, a little rumpled from the drive from London. His racy Porsche was parked at the gate of Summer Cottage.

'Surprised to see me?' In one hand he held a bottle of wine, a bunch of bright yellow chrysanthemums in the other. 'Hope you like 'em, whatever they are,' he said, waving them like a sword. 'All I could find at the local cemetery.'

'Chester?'

He glanced at her pyjamas. 'Kind of late in the day to have just got up. You're not ill, are you? You look – what is it you Brits say? *Out of sorts.*'

She did feel slightly weird. Dazed, unfocused. 'I've been … working on something,' she said hesitantly. 'Didn't have time to change.'

'Great to hear you're keeping busy. Aren't you going to ask me in?'

'Of course. I'm sorry. Come inside.'

He hefted his boxy frame into the hall. 'So this is where the great Ellen Grace once lived, huh? Wow. Feel like I'm stepping back into literary history. Not that I thought she could write worth a damn.'

She scowled at him, then hurried upstairs, grabbed a dressing gown and came back down tying up the sash belt. 'Why are you here, Chester?'

Her question was sharp, but Chester was impervious to taking offence. Pressing the flowers and the bottle into her hands, he said, 'One reason I'm here is to give you these and say I'm sorry if I gave you the hard talk yesterday. I felt bad about it afterwards. Anyway, I happened to be passing through the area, so—'

'It's all right, Chester. I'm used to your ways. Thanks for the wine and flowers.'

'You're definitely okay? You look kind of pale.'

'It's nothing.'

'Pleased to hear it. I need my writers firing on all cylinders.'

'For what it's worth.'

'You never can tell. The other reason I'm here is, I have a proposition for you. Go make me a coffee. Strong, black, four sugars. I'm dying. Then I'll tell you what I've got.'

She went into the kitchen, laid the wine and the flowers aside and made the coffee, wondering what he'd come up with. As the percolator began to bubble up she heard his voice from the hallway saying, 'So this here must be the engine room, huh?' followed by the creak of the study door opening and his footsteps going inside.

'Uh, yeah, that's right. ' she called back. 'Did you say *four* sugars?'

He didn't reply. 'That's disgusting,' she muttered to herself. She grabbed a small plate from the cupboard, spilled a few ginger biscuits onto it and carried it through, together with the appallingly oversweetened coffee, into her writing study.

'Now tell me—' she began.

The agent was sitting at her desk, his heavy shape bent over her computer, staring avidly at the screen.

'Chester, do you mind? That's my private—'

'Shhh,' he said, waving an arm at her, not taking his eyes off what he was hungrily reading.

'What are you looking at?'

'This is unbelievable,' he muttered.

She strode over to the computer and saw with stupefaction that he had in front of him the work she'd done that morning. How could it be? 'Jesus, you're not supposed to see this. I thought I'd deleted it.'

'I'm glad you didn't,' he said, almost laughing with pleasure. 'How long have you been working on this? It's mind-blowing.'

'Just since this morning,' she said sheepishly.

'There's nearly ten thousand words here. You telling me you wrote all that *today?*'

'Look, it's rubbish, Chester. I don't know why it's even still there. I was positive I'd binned it. Now I will for sure.'

'Uh –uh. I don't want you to bin it. I want you to go on with it.'

'*What?*'

'Have you any idea how big a market there is for this kind of schlocky stuff?' he asked. 'You write me another ten k like this and I can sell it on a partial. I already know who to go to. Believe me, I'll have a bidding war going before you know it.'

'I don't know if I can.'

'It's in you. It'll come out. Trust me.' He drained his mug at a single huge gulp. 'Hmm. Great coffee. Now I guess I'll be on my way. Don't want to stem the creative flow, and all that jazz. I *was* going to tell you about this proposal—'

'What was it?'

'Just a co-writing project with another author,' he said dismissively.

'Who?'

'Jenny.' Jenny Stickle was one of Chester's stable of clients, a writer so overpaid and jaded that she now barely contributed a word to her own novels. "Co-authoring" with her basically meant doing all the donkey work under her haughty eye, and was regarded as a step up for flagging mid-listers.

'I'm not that desperate,' Mandy said.

'Forget I mentioned it. You're too good for the old bitch anyway. Especially now that this has come up.' He stood. 'Back to the desk, kiddo. Enjoy the vino. Don't forget to put the flowers in water.'

Before she could say anything or try to stop him, he was striding out of the front door and back to his Porsche.

SEVEN

IT WAS WITH a lot of trepidation that Mandy returned to the manuscript that afternoon. She couldn't understand why it had remained on her computer. She *knew* she'd deleted the file before Chester had turned up. Killed it, obliterated it.

But it had come back. As if it didn't want to die. As if it wanted to be written, and had chosen her to be its channel.

She was so disgusted by what she'd written that she could hardly bear to read it, let alone consciously come up with more of it. And yet, as she put her fingers to the keys, out of nowhere the flood resumed. Locking her mind into itself, making it impossible to stop.

Mandy wrote until the study windows were in darkness and the only light in the room was the glow of her screen. Only then did she feel as if she'd been released. The word count now read 19,758, almost a quarter of a full length manuscript. It took her breath away to think she'd done this.

Wearily, her eyes burning, she staggered to the kitchen and ate a sandwich that barely seemed to taste of anything.

She dragged herself upstairs for a shower, then pulled on jeans and a sweater. In the entrance hall she grabbed the torch, stepped into her pair of Wellingtons and called Buster out into the cold evening for his walk. The dog seemed unusually glad to escape the confines of Summer Cottage.

Crossing the dark meadow behind the house and listening to the whisper of the trees that lined its edges, Mandy shivered and flicked torchlight here and there into shadows that looked alive and moving, only to see bushes and dying leaves rustling in the wind. 'You're scaring yourself,' she said with a nervous chuckle. After a few minutes she called Buster back, and had to coax him to return to the house.

She'd willed herself not to go straight back to the computer, but there it sat, calling her. She wrote until midnight and then trudged upstairs to bed, too exhausted even to think. The moment her head touched the pillow she was ready to fall into a deep and instant sleep.

But when she did, the nightmares quickly returned. Horrific nebulous figures that seemed to swirl and swim around her, taunting her with whispering voices. The creeping certainty that there was something, someone, in the room with her, breathing on her and running icy cold fingers down her face.

Then she was wandering through the darkness of Summer Cottage, walking the passage that led from the hallway past the kitchen and her study and onwards through the house. Her bare feet shambled forwards as if in trance as a strange greenish-yellow glow led her through the winding passage, seeming to lure her on step by step. Shadows flitting all around her. Perspectives distorted as if through a lens. Deeper and deeper into the house, the passageway narrowing until the walls, now dank and dripping and mottled with black mould, brushed her shoulders as she walked.

Ahead of her, the yellowish glow seemed to emanate from a half-open doorway. She knew the source of the light lay beyond. The voices were calling for her to join them there.

She saw her hand reach out to the door, but before her fingers touched it, it swung open as if of its own accord. The light was brighter down there, drifting like a thick mist. The whispers spoke more loudly inside her head.

Then, a low, chittering cackle. Frightened, she tried to pull away from the light, but found it drawing her towards it like a magnetic field of invisible power. She didn't want to go there. The voice filled her head until it felt it could split apart. Her mouth gaped open in a silent scream.

Crash.

Mandy's eyes snapped open. She was covered in sweat. Her bedcovers were thrown back. She'd been thrashing about in the throes of her nightmare and knocked over her bedside table lamp.

Breathing hard, she swung her legs out of the bed, picked up the fallen lamp and tried the switch. It was working, and she was deeply grateful for the light. She left it on and crawled back into bed, afraid to close her eyes. Too tired and drained to go downstairs the way she'd done the night before, she just lay there staring at the ceiling until dawn.

The first thing she did the next morning, before she'd brewed her coffee or even let Buster out into the garden, was to revisit the passage downstairs. She paced its length, trying to remember the way it had been in her dreams. It was all so different now, sunlight streaming in through the small leaded window-panes and dappling on the walls, which were far enough apart for her to extend both arms full-length without her stretched-out fingers touching them. Where in the dream the passage had led to a door, there was only a solid wall. She tapped it with her knuckles, listening for any kind of hollow resonance. Nothing but thick stone. Foolish to imagine it would have been anything else.

Pull yourself together, girl. You're losing it. It was just a stupid nightmare. Writing all this horror shit is getting to you.

Fighting to shake the memory from her mind, she returned to the kitchen to make her coffee, attend to Buster and face up to the day ahead. In a water-filled jug on the kitchen worktop were the flowers Chester had brought her, now all curled up and brown, looking as if they'd been left neglected there for weeks. 'Wonder what filling station you bought those in, Chester.'

She thought about the white roses that Sarah Grace had left her as a welcoming gift, and how fast they'd seemed to die, too. Strange. Maybe the cottage, with its thick walls and small windows, just wasn't suited to flowers.

She was tossing the wilted chrysanthemums in the bin when she heard the phone.

Chester again, sounding as if he was bubbling with excitement. Mandy's eyebrows rose. Nobody had ever seen or heard Chester bubbling with excitement, unless it was a million-pound publishing deal.

'It's great! Great! Fantastic!' he kept repeating.

'What is?' she said blankly.

'The sample, the sample. I mean, wow! Just *wow!* It's sadistic, it's cruel, it's morbid, it's vicious, it's twisted, it's wonderful! I fucking love it! You hear me? If I'd known you could write like this, I'd have got you out of doing that romantic slush years ago. You have a title yet? I had some ideas we could throw around otherwise.'

'Hold on, Chester. I don't know what you're talking about. What sample?'

'Are you suffering from amnesia or something? The sample you emailed me. It hit my inbox at four in the morning. I got into the office an hour ago and I've been reading it ever since, all twenty thousand-plus words of it.'

'But I—'

'I just came off the phone with Norris Elliot at Pan, and before that I was talking to Melanie Rothwell at Penguin's new horror imprint, DarkNite. They're both hot for it. Of course, I haven't told them who the author is. I'm letting them dangle for now. All they know is, it's from a debut writer who's gonna blow everyone's socks off and pull a high six-figure advance. Easy.'

'But Chester, I never emailed anyth—' she tried to say.

Chester went on talking, running over her like an express train. He was in full piratical mode now, buzzing with the thrill of the thing he loved most: the colour of publishers' money. 'But I'll have to throw them a name before long if we want to close a deal. Oh, listen – someone's on the other line. Could be one of our fishes biting. Got to go. Don't stop what you're doing. Work! Work! Send me more as soon as you got it!' He hung up.

Mandy's head was reeling after the call. She hurried into the study to check her computer and, sure enough, the 22,000 word sample had been emailed to Chester from her account just after four a.m. She could not remember having done it. Was she going mad?

Returning to the kitchen she felt badly in need of a drink. As a rule she never boozed alone, and certainly not in the morning – but now she craved something stronger than coffee. She opened the wine Chester had brought and poured herself a large glass, slumping at the table to gulp it down.

That was when she noticed Buster. He was cringing near the back door, as if afraid of something. 'What is it, boy?' she asked him, frowning. She put down her wineglass, stood up and went over to him.

He whimpered. 'What's the matter with you?' She knelt down beside him, running her hand down the coarse fur of his back.

She stopped as a sound came through the wall. An electric jolt of alarm shot through her heart.

There it was again.

Someone was inside the cottage. In her dining room, playing her piano.

EIGHT

NO, NOT PLAYING it. What was coming from the dining room wasn't music. It was a jarring dissonant noise from keys being depressed randomly up and down the octaves. A crashing rumble of bass notes; a pause; then the spine-chilling tinkle of the upper range.

Mandy's whole body was rigid with tension as she tore open a drawer and grabbed a carving knife. 'Stay,' she hissed at the frightened dog. She crept out into the passage and approached the closed dining room door.

'Hello?' Her voice came out as a croak. 'Who's there?' she demanded in a stronger tone. 'Who the hell is that?'

There was no reply. The noise of the piano went on. It could have been a child banging on the keys. Or music played by a madman.

Her mouth was dry. She paused outside the door, listening for a moment; then with a shaking hand she reached for the doorknob.

Turned it— Softly, gently—

Mandy edged through the doorway, heart thumping. She didn't know what she was going to find. Her fingers gripped the knife handle.

She let out a cry of fear and shock as a large black shape threw itself down from the top of the piano and darted towards her.

A cat. A big black cat with a white tip to its tail.

Mandy almost collapsed with relief. The hand clutching the long carving knife fell limp at her side.

The cat slunk quickly out of the open door and into the passage, like an escaping thief.

'So you must be Dinky bloody Dora,' Mandy shouted after it, remembering what that old loony Danvers had said. 'How the hell did you get in here? Shoo! Away with you!' She chased it towards the entrance, opened the front door, and the cat bolted off with a last wild and indignant stare.

Mandy closed the door hard and stood leaning with her back against it, breathing hard from the fright the damn thing had given her. It must have sneaked in an open window and got trapped in the room somehow. She couldn't remember having left a window open. But then, she couldn't remember having emailed Chester at four in the morning either.

'I must be losing my mind.' Legs like jelly, she walked back towards the kitchen still clutching the carving knife. 'What about you?' she said to Buster as she slammed the knife back inside the drawer. 'You're supposed to be a guard dog, not petrified of some old witch lady's cat.'

Buster just looked at her.

For the next three days, Mandy closed herself in Summer Cottage and wrote, and wrote, and wrote more. It was compulsive. When she wasn't eating or sleeping or seeing to Buster's needs, she was writing. As though she simply *had* to. She felt guilty about disconnecting the phone, in case Todd tried to call her and wondered why she was ignoring him – but she couldn't be distracted. The only interruption to her routine was the visit from the telecom engineer she'd arranged to have come and install a landline extension in her bedroom, as mobiles refused to work at Summer Cottage.

Her days become a numbing cycle. Writing. Sparse, desultory meals alone in the kitchen. Back to writing. Then bed; and in the night the dreams would return, making it impossible for her to snatch more than a few hours' troubled sleep.

The dreams were always the same. She saw the doorway up the passage, the mysterious light beyond it drawing her in deeper, a little deeper each time. When she awoke, the temptation to seek out the place where she'd dreamed the door was became stronger each passing morning. She had to keep telling herself: 'There is no door. It's only dreams. Just a phase you're going through or something. It'll pass.'

The lure of the writing desk, though, was irresistible. The hours would tumble past. Day merged into night. The developing book manuscript grew ever longer. She experienced its steady growth almost like a physical sensation, like something alive that she could feel swelling and pulsating under the light pressure of her fingers on the laptop keys.

Finally, incredibly, the book was finished. When she hit the final full stop it was early afternoon and she'd gone without any breakfast or lunch. She slumped back in her chair, exhausted, dizzy from concentration and lack of sleep, her eyes feeling gritty and raw, fingers numb from typing.

She still had no title and no pen-name.

Instants later, as from nowhere, both leapt into her mind. She leaned back over the keyboard, scrolled right back to the front of the document and wrote in large bold font:

ORGASM OF BLOOD
By
Jessica Lomax

She stared at the new title page. 'Did I really just write that?' But she had, just like she'd written the other ninety thousand stomach-churning words that she couldn't have imagined herself capable of dreaming up.

High six-figure deal, Chester had said. He'd sounded super-confident. Like it was already a done thing.

She looked around the room at her scanty furniture, the cheap self-assembly desk, the threadbare armchair. She thought of how fine Summer Cottage's interiors must have looked when the wealthy Ellen Grace had been its owner.

And she wondered.

'You want to call it *what?*' Chester virtually shouted over the phone when she called him later that afternoon.

She told him again. 'Don't you like it?'

'I love it, but I'm not sure the publishers will.'

'I've been thinking, Chester. Screw the publishers.'

He sounded as if he'd been punched in the guts. 'What are you saying?' he wheezed. 'I've got Pan, DarkNite and now Vince Pratt at Hodder all ready to wade through a lake of pus to acquire this thing and you want to *pull out?*'

'Who said anything about pulling out? I'm not giving this to a publisher, that's all.'

'The money's virtually on the table, Mandy.'

'I'm going to self publish this,' she said.

'*What?*'

'Ebook only. To hell with the publishers, they're a bunch of parasites.'

'Yeah, sure, parasites with lots and lots of cash. They're like spoilt, useless rich kids with more money rolling in than they know what to do with. But who cares? Think of the advance. The bidding's already up to three-eighty. Your third up front on signature is—'

'I can count. No more games with these people,' she said firmly. 'Most of the editors can't edit, some of them can't even spell.'

'They'll get you someone better—'

'They talk up a storm about promotion and don't deliver on their promises.'

'They'll promote the crap out of this one, I'll make sure of it personally!' Chester protested. She could picture his face turning purple as he clutched the phone.

'Do you know any editor who's ever written a book?' she said.

'No …'

'I mean, in what other profession would you be expected to take orders from someone who's never actually done it? Can you imagine a mechanic taking advice from someone who's never even changed a car wheel, or a surgeon having to defer to someone who's never performed an operation?'

'Come on, Mandy, you know the score. This is the publishing biz.'

'Yeah. Exactly. And I'm expected to hand over ninety percent to these jokers, in return for what? Forget it, Chester. I'm going solo.'

'I can't believe I'm hearing this. This isn't mild-mannered Mandy Freeman the romantic novelist talking. Where's this ballsy new attitude coming from?'

'I don't really know,' she admitted. 'I feel sort of different.'

'Different?'

'You've always stood by me. You'll still get your commission, if that's what you're worried about.'

'Well ...'

'Trust me, Chester. This way, we don't have to sit around waiting six months or even longer while the editors fiddle about getting the book out there. Arguing over titles, wasting time over "wouldn't it be cool" plotting ideas that don't work. We'll get this out in a week, or less even. Straight out to the readers. Jessica Lomax has arrived.'

'What about the cover? Who's going to take care of the design?' Chester said, defeated.

'I've already thought of that,' she told him.

NINE

THE PAIR MET that night in the Fox and Hounds in Fairwood. Todd got up from his seat near the crackling log fire when he saw Mandy walk into the crowded pub. They kissed hesitantly, like nervous teenagers. He squeezed her hand and looked at her with concern. 'Are you all right?'

'Why shouldn't I be?'

'You've lost weight, you look drained, you've got dark circles under your eyes … '

'Thanks. Just the look I was going for,' she said with a tight smile.

'No offence. It's just you look absolutely knackered. You're not ill, are you? Here, come and sit where it's warm.'

She sat with him by the fire. 'Really, I'm fine,' she insisted. In truth, the dizziness that had come on after finishing the book was still lingering, leaving a slightly nauseous feeling. She felt odd, strangely detached somehow. 'Been working hard the last few days, that's all,' she added. 'That's why I didn't answer the phone.'

'I tried calling about a hundred times. I'd have come round in person, but I've been so busy myself, and on the road. That shoot up in Scotland I told you about.'

Her mind had been so filled with her writing that she had to make an effort to remember. 'How did it go?'

He shrugged. 'Oh, you know. Nothing special, just some shots for a posh golf club website. Weather was glorious. But never mind that. Let me get you a drink. You look like you need one.'

The only variety of red wine they served in the Fox and Hounds was a thick-tasting syrup the colour of blood, but Mandy sipped it gratefully as they sat close together by the crackling fire. 'Listen, Todd, I need your help. Your professional help, that is.'

'I'm intrigued. Let me guess, you want a photo of yourself outside Summer Cottage, like Ellen Grace's picture?'

She shook her head. 'No, I need you to design a cover for the book I'm working on. Can you do that?'

'I'm pretty good with graphic design, Photoshop and stuff. Sure. But don't publishers have departments to do all that for writers?'

She explained her plan to go indie. Even more intrigued, he asked her what she was writing about, and she told him.

'Horror?'

'I know, it's a departure. Came as a surprise to me, too. Just kind of crept up on me.'

'That sounds appropriate to the genre, I suppose. How long's it going to take to write it?'

She shrugged. 'It's already done. Finished it in a week.'

His mouth gaped open. 'A week? Well, that explains the circles under the eyes. You can't do that to yourself, Mandy. It's not healthy.'

'Can you help?' she asked. 'I'd need it really soon, so I can get the ebook out there as fast as possible. I'll pay you.'

'Hey, no money talk, not between us,' he warned her gently. 'I suppose I'd need to read it, to spark off a few visual ideas?'

'No need for you to read it,' she said quickly. 'We can discuss ideas.'

'Scared I'll get too many insights into your darker side?' he said with a smile.

'I'm scared of it myself.'

After a few more drinks, Todd invited her back to his place on Fairwood's Main Street, just walking distance from the pub. 'Not tonight, Todd,' she said. That feeling of nausea still hadn't gone away, and as close as she wanted to get to Todd, she somehow felt the urge to get back to Summer Cottage.

'I didn't mean—' he began, then flushed.

'Nor did I.' She gave a weak smile. 'I'll see you soon, all right?'

'Are you sure you're all right, Mandy?'

'I'll be fine. Just need a good night's sleep. Alone.'

'That's a hint I can take,' he said ruefully.

'I like you, Todd. I mean it. A lot.'

'I'll call you,' he said.

She nodded, kissed him and went to her car.

As Mandy drove home through the dark lanes, drops of the first rainfall since her move to Fairwood speckled the Kia's windscreen. The trees seemed to loom over the road ahead, and a prickly sensation of anxiety nagged at her mind. What's wrong with you, she asked herself. You found your haven here in this place. And you found a man you could settle with, maybe. You should be so happy.

Life is good. Isn't it?

But the feeling wouldn't go away.

As she reached Summer Cottage, the warm glow from the windows glimmered through the branches. Crime was by all accounts pretty much nonexistent in and around Fairwood, but for security reasons she liked to leave lights on when she went out in the evening, to give the impression someone was at home, and for the comfort of returning to a lit-up house.

Buster didn't greet her at the front door, the way he normally would have. If the little guy didn't perk up soon, she'd have to call the vet. She fed him a snack and then let him out into the back garden for a few minutes while she made her nightly mug of cocoa. Then she closed up the house and climbed the stairs. Her legs felt heavy as she walked down the long, brightly-illuminated corridor that led to her bedroom, clicking off the old-fashioned switches of the wall lights as she went.

The rain was falling harder now, pittering slantwise against the bedroom windows as she shut the curtains, undressed and got into her pyjamas. She slipped under the duvet with her Ellen Grace novel, but not even immersing herself in the cosy fiction world created by her idol was enough to keep her eyelids from drooping. It wasn't long before she turned off the light and nuzzled into the soft feather pillow.

Please don't let the dreams come again tonight, she prayed. She felt so exhausted in mind and body, it seemed to her instead that she'd tumble into a black hole and sleep the sleep of the dead until dawn came. It was a comforting final thought before she let herself begin to drift off.

Sleep came over her like a soft blanket.

Then her eyes flew open in the darkness. Her senses suddenly jangling. Too tense to breathe.

She knew what it was she'd just heard. The distinct *clunk* of one of the corridor light switches being flipped.

This was no dream. She was not alone in the cottage.

TEN

MANDY FOUGHT THE urge to dive under the bedclothes. Her frozen gaze locked on to the bedroom door: a moment earlier its shape had been lost in the pitch blackness of the room; now it stood faintly outlined by a glimmer of light.

Then, the unmistakable sound of a muffled footstep beyond the thick oak door. Followed by a second click as another of the corridor lights was switched on.

Closer now. The thin strip of light around the bedroom door a little brighter.

Horror welled up like bile in Mandy's throat. Galvanised by her panic, she leaped out of bed and ran to the door, slapping on the main bedroom light switch on the wall next to it. The sudden intense brightness of the room made her blink. She grasped the ring of the iron door key and twisted it, locking herself in.

She backed away from the door, breathless and shaking. 'Who's there?' she demanded in a quavering voice. 'I said, who's there?'

The only reply was another shuffling footstep from

outside in the corridor. There came another click as the closest of the three wall lights was switched on.

In her mind she involuntarily pictured the hand turning on the light. Skeletal fingers caressing the switch. Taking their time. The scrape of cold bone. The mental image made her want to scream.

Whoever or whatever was out there, it was now standing right outside her door. All that separated them were three inches of oak. How easily could the door be broken down? How strong was the old lock?

'Whoever you are, you'd better leave now,' she shouted. Her voice was shaking so badly, the words came out half garbled. 'I have a phone in here and I'm calling for help!'

Still no reply. Mandy ventured a step closer to the door. Then another. Trembling, she pressed an ear to the smooth wood.

And thought she could hear raspy breathing on the other side as the intruder hovered there. Waiting. Waiting for what?

The doorknob turned. Gently at first. Then with more force.

Mandy recoiled from the door in fright. She clutched her side of the knob, gripping it tightly with both hands and trying to prevent it from turning, but she lacked the strength and it twisted violently back and forth in her fingers. 'Leave me alone!' she screamed.

An impact against the door made the oak shudder in its frame. Then another blow, harder, resonating through the floorboards so that they quivered under her bare feet. Mandy let go of the knob and backed away, thinking desperately of escape. The door began to rattle with increasing violence, building into a frenzy so intense that she was certain it would rip from its hinges with an explosion of splintering oak.

And if that happened, what would follow?

Everything in the bedroom seemed to be shaking. She could hear Buster downstairs, barking and howling like a crazed wild animal.

The door went on shaking. For a few instants, Mandy seriously considered jumping from the window. But what if she only succeeded in injuring herself? How could she escape from her intruder with a broken ankle or leg?

She ran to the phone extension at her bedside and snatched up the receiver. Her hands were trembling so badly she could barely dial in Todd's number. When he answered, she screamed into the phone, 'Todd! Todd! Someone's in the cottage! They're outside my bedroom door! Help me! Please!'

'Hold on, Mandy, I'm coming!' Todd's voice said on the line.

'Hurry!'

The line went dead. At that precise instant, the insane rattling at the door fell into complete silence.

Slowly, hardly daring to, Mandy looked back at the door. The strip of light underneath it seemed to have disappeared, but with the bedroom lit up it was hard to tell.

She crept nervously to the doorway and turned off the main bedroom light.

In darkness, too terrified to breathe, she crouched down in front of the keyhole, felt for the cold iron ring and drew out the key as quietly as she could. Peering through the keyhole, she saw only the solid blackness of the empty corridor.

Whatever had been out there was now gone.

A few minutes seemed like hours before the reflection of car headlights swept the bedroom window and she faintly heard the sound of Todd's Volvo rasping to a halt on the lane outside the gate. A door opening, closing; then a few moments later, running footsteps coming round to the back of the house. Mandy rushed to the window and ripped open the curtain to see a shining light and the dark figure of Todd standing there, torch in one hand, something that looked like a cricket bat in the other. She unlocked the window and threw it open. 'Todd! Thank Christ!'

'No windows smashed,' he called up to her. 'Your front door's locked, so's the back. Nobody seems to be about. Let me in.'

'Are you sure?' she called back down to him, terrified to open her door in case the intruder might still be lurking there. She had to summon all her courage to turn the key and slowly, slowly, creak open the door. The darkness of the corridor seemed to waft into the bedroom like a smell.

The nearest corridor light was just a foot away. She clicked it on, then ventured as far as the next, chasing away the darkness. The corridor was empty.

She crept anxiously down the stairs. Buster was still barking inside the kitchen. Mandy turned on the lights, ran to the front door, unlocked it.

'Are you all right?' Todd asked grimly, stepping into the entrance hall. He laid down the long metal torch he was carrying, shut the door behind him and gripped her hand. There was mud on his shoes where he'd run from the car in the pouring rain. He wiped them clean on the mat.

She was almost crying with relief. 'Todd, I didn't dream it. Someone was here!'

'Are you hurt? Did he touch you?'

'I locked myself in the bedroom. He tried to get inside. Then just as I phoned you, he was gone!'

'Let's take a look,' he said firmly, clutching her hand tightly in his, cricket bat ready. She was glad of his strength. 'Ground floor first,' he said.

They opened the kitchen door and Buster burst out, yapping frenziedly with his tail tight between his legs. 'Look at him,' Mandy said as she tried to calm the dog. 'I've never seen him so nervous.'

As they checked each room in turn, she described in a shaky voice exactly what had happened, from the beginning. 'You have to believe me. Someone was here.'

Todd said nothing until they'd checked every room in the cottage. Finally, he turned to her. 'Mandy, there's no sign of any intruder having been here. Are you really certain you didn't just imagine it?'

'Yes! I—'

'Please, listen. Let's be logical about this. It's pissing with rain outside. The front path and garden are all muddy. If someone had got in here, they'd have left a trail of footsteps across the hallway, up the stairs, along the passage to your bedroom. But there's nothing. How did they get in? And who would break into a place where there's a dog barking its head off?'

'But—'

'I know it's hard to accept, but isn't it possible you just had a nightmare?'

'It was real! It happened!'

'Maybe it only seemed real,' Todd said. 'Especially for an overimaginative writer living all alone in an old house, with a head full of horror stories. A writer who's written a whole novel in a week, driving herself half nuts with overwork, and probably hasn't been eating properly.'

Mandy stared at him. Her lip began to tremble.

'Don't be angry with me, Mandy,' he implored her. 'Please. I care deeply about you.'

She burst into tears and fell into his arms. 'Oh, Todd, please don't go away tonight. Please, stay with me.'

'Of course I will,' he replied, holding her. 'Get me a blanket and I'll kip on the sofa.'

She looked at him with wide, wet eyes. 'No,' she said. 'I mean *stay* with me. I want you with me tonight.'

ELEVEN

AS THEY SAT at breakfast the next morning, Mandy and Todd couldn't stop glancing at one another and breaking into smiles. She'd slept soundly that night, all right, though not quite for the reason she'd initially thought when she'd gone to bed alone. For the first time in days there was a rosy glow in her cheeks.

'I like to see you eating with appetite,' Todd said. 'It's what you need.'

'Now, I wonder why it could be that I'm so hungry,' she said, and her smile widened. They held hands across the table, leaned closer and kissed.

'Listen, I had an idea for your book cover,' he said, buttering another slice of toast. 'If you're still up for me doing it, that is.'

'Of course. Tell me.'

'Oh, I can do better than that. I can show you.'

In her study after breakfast, she stood next to him as he sat at her computer and logged onto a password-protected online storage facility where he backed up a lot of his photographic images. 'Now let's see ... there it is.'

'You've already done it?' she asked, amazed.

'More or less. Just needs a bit of touching up. Assuming you like it, of course.'

'When on earth did you find the time?'

'I like to work fast, and work late. It's what I was doing when you called me last night.' He opened up the PDF file. 'Et voilá. Now, be honest.'

Mandy looked at the image on the screen, and gasped.

'You hate it, don't you?' he said, seeing her wide-eyed expression.

The image showed a grinning decapitated skull with the handle of a cutthroat razor protruding from its empty eye socket. The title and the name Jessica Lomax screamed out from the page, in stark, blood-red Gothic script.

'Hate it? I think it's brilliant. It's exactly what I'd imagined.' Which, she thought uncomfortably, was disturbing in itself.

Todd looked pleased. 'Now, you remember I was telling you about that Cornwall shoot I have coming up? Well, the client called and it's been brought forward, but I still have a couple of free days before I leave. Gives me time for other things I want to do with you.'

'Do tell,' she said, raising her eyebrows, leaning her elbows on the desk with her chin on her hands.

He grinned. 'Well, that too. But I was talking about your new image.'

'New image?'

'You have a new persona now, so you need a new look. Give the right kind of impression for the Jessica Lomax website.'

'But there isn't a—'

'There soon will be. I'm going to build it for you.'

Later that morning, Todd fetched a couple of aluminium cases full of lighting equipment that he kept in his car, and set up a makeshift photography studio in the living room of Summer Cottage. Mandy did her own makeup and hair and put on a black dress, and for a couple of hours they experimented to get the ideal shot of the new author, Jessica Lomax. The end result was a striking series of shady, moody images of an unrecognisable Mandy with her black hair covering half her face, her one visible eye heavily made up to look as little as possible like the Mandy Freeman her regular readers knew. The lips were startling red, her cheek and neck as white as chalk. With a few digital embellishments added at the computer, Todd managed to make her look deathly and sexy at the same time. It was the perfect image. Jessica Lomax was suddenly a reality.

'Not a bad morning's work,' he said, looking at his watch. 'Now, to make a perfect day even better, I'm going to run out to the village and get us some goodies for lunch.'

'Sounds wonderful. Meanwhile, I'm going up to scrub all this makeup off me and change into some proper clothes.'

'Shame. I kind of like you like that.'

She nudged him. 'Pervert. Listen, grab the spare front door key off the hook in the hall, will you? In case I'm still in the bathroom when you get back.'

Upstairs, she hummed a little tune to herself as she crossed the bedroom. She smiled coyly at the sight of the rumpled bed and the recent memories it evoked. After her night with Todd she'd managed to virtually forget what had happened before. She was willing to believe he'd been right – that what she'd experienced had been some kind of waking dream concocted by an anxious mind. It was very possible, she'd decided, that all this had been brought on by the shock of being dropped by her publisher. Stress could play all kinds of malevolent tricks. She resolved to take it easier from now on.

From the window she watched Todd's Volvo snaking away up the road towards Fairwood. Last night's deluge had given way to another radiant autumnal morning. Buster was outside in the garden, foraging near the hedge and looking happy enough. Maybe he didn't need to see a vet after all, thank God.

Feeling buoyant, Mandy went into the ensuite bathroom, leaving the door ajar. She took her time changing out of the black dress and back into her regular uniform of jeans and jumper. Taking a little bottle of makeup remover and a packet of cotton balls from the bathroom cupboard, she stepped across to the mirror over the washbasin and started dabbing away the eye makeup. When she was starting to look like her normal self again, she reached for a brush and began rearranging her long black hair to the way she usually wore it.

She paused, sensing a presence in the bedroom behind her. In the mirror's reflection, she thought she saw a flitting movement through the gap in the slightly-open bathroom door.

'Todd?' She put down the brush with a smile and turned away from the basin, heading back into the bedroom. 'You were quick. What goodies have you got us this t—'

She stopped. Glanced around the room. Todd wasn't there. And yet, she was sure she'd seen someone.

The bedroom door lay open through to the corridor beyond. Mandy's smile faltered as last night's frightening events began to creep back into her memory. A cold shiver made her rub her arms, pushing her hands up inside the loose sleeves of her jumper to feel the goosebumps that had appeared on her skin. 'Todd?' she called out, walking into the corridor and along towards the stairs. Her legs suddenly felt stiff, her gait jerky.

Bang!

The sound of the door slamming somewhere downstairs felt as loud as a rifle shot and made her jump. The crash seemed to resonate through the whole of Summer Cottage, shaking its ancient timbers from end to end.

She paused at the top of the stairs, peering down, trying to control the creeping terror that was spreading through her.

Another sound. What was that? For an instant she tensed even more, then realised that it was the sound of Todd's car returning. Her heart gave a little leap and she started down the stairs to meet him.

The front door opened and Todd stepped cheerfully into the entrance hall, clutching a bulging grocery bag. 'Got us some beautiful lemon sole fillets from Sparrowhawks the fishmonger,' he called out. 'Bunch of fresh parsley, lemon, butter, baguette and an organic salad. Hope you're hungry.'

Mandy tried to smile as she came down the stairs. She could hide the tremors in her hands and knees, but not the look on her face.

'What's wrong?'

'Nothing,' she said stiffly.

He put down the grocery bag and came towards her with his arms outstretched. 'Come on. What is it?'

'Thought I saw someone,' she said, avoiding his embrace.

Todd drew back. His face fell. 'Someone? Where?'

'Here in the cottage. In … in the bedroom. Just a moment ago.'

'*Again?*'

'I didn't really get a good look. Just a movement. A shadow.'

'Christ, Mandy. It was … I don't know. Probably Buster running about the place. Chasing mice or something.'

She shook her head, arms folded across her chest. 'Buster's in the garden. It wasn't him I saw. It was a figure.'

'A figure.'

She nodded. 'Then a door slammed.'

'What door?'

'Somewhere downstairs. Sounded like a bloody gun going off.'

'What are you so frightened of? It was just a door slamming.'

She shook her head again. 'Todd. I don't know how to say this … there's something not right here.'

'What's that supposed to mean?'

'Here, here in this place, this house. There's something …' She couldn't finish the sentence. Glanced nervously about her.

'For Christ's sake, Mandy, you need to get past this,' he said, frowning at her. 'There's nobody here except us. What makes you think any different?'

'I don't know, Todd. I only know that you don't believe me.'

He passed a hand over his face. 'Look, I got us some good wine, lots of lovely ingredients. It'll take me exactly fifteen minutes to cook up the best fast food you've ever tasted. Sit down, put your feet up, I'll pour you a glass of wine—'

'I'm not hungry,' she said.

'Because of a banging door?' he said, beginning to look exasperated.

Mandy said nothing.

'That's ridiculous,' Todd said.

'No. It's not.'

He sighed. 'Yes, it is, and let me show you why. How about I explain the mystery of the banging door, once and for all?' He held out his hand, fingers reaching for hers. 'Come on.'

Tentatively, she took his hand. He led her across the entrance hall to the closed living room door, opened it and motioned at the empty room beyond. 'Nobody there, see? Now, do you notice the open window? I opened it before I left, because the warmth from the lighting gear had made the room stuffy. Must have caused a draught. Door slams. Case solved. Now let's eat. Please.'

She shook her head. Tears had formed in her eyes and one rolled down her cheek. 'No, Todd, you can't explain it all away so easily. What about the figure I saw just now?'

'How can you be so sure that's what you saw?'

'What about last night?'

'Last night was just—'

'And what about my dreams? What about the cellar?'

Todd's face was growing redder. 'There is no cellar, Mandy.'

'I've seen it. I know it's there. It seemed so real.'

'*Seemed*, exactly. So you admit yourself that it's not real!'

'I don't know, Todd. I saw it. The same thing, exactly the same, over and over. The doorway leading to it, and these steps leading down.'

'In your *dreams* …'

'And this light. This horrible light …'

'Where?'

'Now it's my turn. I'll show you.' She took his hand and led him down the passage, sensing his reluctance. 'It was here, around the corner.' When she got to the place, she stopped and pointed at the wall. 'There. That's where I saw it.'

'Yeah, in a dream,' he said again, staring at her as if she were insane.

'Don't look at me like that. It was there.'

'How could it be there, for God's sake?' he said, shaking his head in disbelief. He banged on the wall. 'See? Solid. If I hit it any harder I'd break my bloody knuckles on it. It's like rock. There's nothing behind this, no hidden doorway, no secret passages. It's a wall, Mandy. It's a *wall*.'

'Fine, so I'm irrational. What my mother says about writers is all true.'

'Or maybe you should just go back to writing historical romances, instead of frightening yourself by conjuring up all these horrors in your head.'

'Says the guy who can dream up skulls with razor blades hanging out of their eyes,' she countered.

'It's just imagination, that's all. I don't let it get to me. Obviously, you do. Come on, Mandy, please. Enough. You're scaring me. This isn't you. This stuff you've been writing is freaky, and it's plainly getting to you.'

She looked at him in surprise. 'You've read it?'

'Some of it, yeah. While you were in the shower, I had a sneak look at it. That was enough for me. It's—' He paused, searching for the right words.

'Spit it out,' she challenged him. 'It's just awful. Total shit. Best thing about it's the cover.'

'I didn't say that. The writing is great. It's the content, Mandy. So *violent*. So dark. Made my stomach churn. I couldn't get past the first few pages.'

'I'm a dark kind of gal,' she said, trying to smile.

'No, you're not. You're a sweet and wonderful woman who's worn herself out by working too hard. That's what I think.'

'Okay, maybe I did wear myself out a bit. But—'

'Maybe nothing,' he insisted. 'It's the truth. You need to relax. Look, let's not argue, okay? Why don't you keep me company in the kitchen while I cook lunch? Everything'll seem different after a glass of this Sauvignon Blanc I got us.'

She sighed, then forced another smile.

'You know I'm right,' he said. He squeezed her hand and gave her that warm, infectious grin that she couldn't resist. The tears were back in her eyes. She wiped them with her sleeve.

'You win. Lead the way, chef,' she said.

Todd's lunch was as delectable as Mandy might have expected. Even so, she never quite relaxed, despite drinking most of the white wine. There was a tense atmosphere in the kitchen as they ate, with Buster curled up in his bed nearby looking miserable and subdued. Their conversation felt forced and she could tell that Todd was perplexed about her behaviour. After lunch, he packed his lighting equipment back into its cases and loaded it into the Volvo, telling her that he was going home to spend the afternoon working on the Jessica Lomax website. 'How about we meet up in the Fox later?' he suggested, and she agreed.

'I want you to rest this afternoon,' he told her. 'Promise me you'll stay away from that damned laptop and take it easy.' His tone was forceful, almost angry, but Mandy understood that behind his emotion was his concern for her.

'Okay, I promise,' she said.

TWELVE

BUT IT WAS a promise soon broken. Too restless to stay away from the computer, Mandy felt herself being drawn back to spend time reading back through the pages of *Orgasm of Blood*.

The strangest thing was that she could now barely remember having written a word of it. 'That's because you didn't,' she said out loud with a bitter chuckle. 'Jessica Lomax did.'

Whatever the case, it was finished. Nothing more could be done except put the thing out live on Amazon and see whether anyone out there would actually want to read it. Closing down the file for the last time, she opened up her new Amazon self-publishing account, went through the file upload procedure, and within minutes the publication process had begun.

'There,' she said. For better or for worse, it was done.

She emailed Chester to tell him, then turned off the computer and finally tore herself away from the desk. There was a sick feeling in her stomach. She didn't feel well, and it wasn't the wine.

She spent a long while staring out of the window. It was getting colder. Autumn was taking a tighter hold over the landscape, trees that had looked golden and radiant in the sunshine just days before now were starting to seem gaunt and bare. The sight somehow made her feel uneasy.

As the afternoon wore on and the sky darkened, all Mandy wanted to do with herself was curl up and sleep. Just to be alone. She regretted having arranged to meet Todd at the pub later. She lay on the sofa, listening to the wind outside the window and the creaking and rattling of the old house all around her.

The dog whimpered in the dark room. She realised she'd forgotten all about his walk, felt rotten about neglecting the poor creature. Forcing herself to get up, she donned her coat and boots, grabbed the torch, and they set off.

The wind drove the mist like smoke across the meadow and blew Mandy's hair over her face and into her eyes as she walked through the long, wet grass. She swept the bobbing torch-beam in front of her, trying to keep Buster in sight as he ran on ahead in the darkness. Seeing him halt to cock his leg on a bush, she took advantage of the pause to gaze back at the dim shape of Summer Cottage, sixty or seventy yards away through the mist.

Despite everything, she told herself, she loved her new home. She needed to be here and would never want to leave.

Uncertainty scratched at the back of her mind as she walked on, but she didn't have time to dwell long on her doubts. Up ahead, Buster suddenly stiffened and then took off in pursuit of something he'd spotted. The torch beam caught a flurry of movement across the dark meadow: a rabbit or a hare, racing off madly through the grass.

Buster tore after it, and in seconds both he and his quarry were lost in the darkness.

Mandy yelled his name, shone the torch this way and that, but couldn't see him. Her fear was that he'd streak right across the fields to the road in the distance and get hit by a car. Cursing, she started running in the direction in which he'd disappeared. The ground was rough; what from her windows looked like a smooth expanse of lush green and wildflowers was in fact full of ruts and rabbit holes, concealed in the long grass and all too easy to stumble over. To make matters worse, the batteries in her torch were beginning to fade, the beam turning a sour sepia yellow in the thickening mist.

'Buster! Come! Buster!'

No sign of him. She stumbled on.

Relief flooded through her moments later as the fading torchlight picked out his little white shape not far ahead. Whether the rabbit had got away from him or whether he'd suddenly lost interest in it, he'd given up the chase and was standing still in the long grass.

Standing very still. Watching something. Fixated, rigid.

As she approached, she saw his whole body was trembling, his tail sticking straight out behind him and quivering like an arrow.

She turned to look in the direction he was staring so intently. And then she saw it, too.

Summer Cottage was shrouded in mist a little over a hundred yards away, its windows glowing amber through the darkness. Mandy's bedroom window was one of the most visible from this spot. The light was on and the curtains open.

A figure stood at the window. Just a shape, silhouetted against the dim light of the room. Looking out.

Looking out at Mandy.

A cold shudder pierced her and made the fading torch tremble in her hand.

Buster began to growl, then to whimper.

A drifting pocket of mist obscured the house for just a moment; when it passed by, the figure had drawn back from the window and could no longer be seen.

It was almost eight-twenty, and Todd was sitting in his usual place near the fire in the Fox and Hounds. He took another sip from his pint of ale, wondering where Mandy was.

He wouldn't have been worried, if she hadn't been acting so strangely. It was beginning to dawn on him how little he really knew this woman: he had to remind himself that they'd only just met. Was she always like this, so highly strung and prone to extreme bouts of nervousness? She might well be, he had to admit to himself.

Todd hated to think it, but he was actually looking forward to his trip to Cornwall, just to get away. It'd be good to have some time apart because, frankly, she was driving him around the twist with all this tension. Was it the stress of moving house, taking on the responsibility of a big place as a single self-employed person with no guaranteed income? Or perhaps it was simply normal behaviour for writers; he'd never known one before, after all. Maybe, he mused, that was just the price they paid for being creative, for delving into the dark recesses of their own minds. God knew there was obviously some dark stuff going on in Mandy's. He'd been more shocked by the content of her new book than he'd been willing to let on.

But, as he fervently hoped, things might settle. For all he knew, when he returned from Cornwall he'd find that her pre-publication nerves, or post-move jitters, or whatever the hell was going on, were done with and she'd get over this weird phase.

It had to be that way. He truly cared about her, and wanted nothing more than for this relationship to survive and develop.

Fifteen more minutes went by before Todd saw her enter the pub. Spotting where he was sitting she hurried over to his table. Right away, he knew that something was up. She looked flushed, flustered and very angry.

'Put down your drink, Todd,' she said breathlessly.

'What are you talking about? Why?'

'Because I want you to come with me. I want you to witness something.'

She was heading for the door before he could say another word, motioning urgently for him to follow. He went after her, bemused. Outside the pub, he saw she'd left her Kia parked on Main Street with the engine still running. The dog was sitting in the back, nose to the glass.

'Get in,' she said to Todd, like a command.

He shook his head. 'First you tell me what this is about. You're acting really odd, Mandy.'

'Trust me. Please. I'm begging you. I need you there.' Her look of rage melted away to one of pleading, and by the light of the streetlamp he could see tears welling up in her eyes. She clutched at his hand, leading him towards the car.

With reluctance, his own annoyance tempered by serious worry about her state of mind, he got into the car. He'd no sooner slammed the passenger door than she threw the Kia into gear and took off, accelerating harshly away up Main Street.

'*Now* will you tell me what's going on?' he asked over the noise of the car. 'What is it you want me to witness, Mandy?'

Silence. Tight-lipped, she sped on towards the outskirts of the village.

'Why won't you answer me? And please slow down. You're driving too fast.'

'We're going to that old bitch Bannister's place.'

'What on earth for?'

'To challenge her. To have it out with her. And I want you to be there. Then you'll know I'm not crazy, Todd.'

'I never said anything about you being crazy!' He could no longer hide the anger in his voice.

'You don't need to,' she said, glancing sideways at him. 'I can see it in your eyes.'

Mandy tore out of Fairwood and on through the winding country lanes, bypassing Summer Cottage. Soon afterwards, she was braking to a screeching halt outside the small, ivy-fronted house where her neighbour lived. 'Here we are,' she fumed, jerking the handbrake and throwing open her door. 'Now for some truth.'

'What truth?' he asked, but she was already out of the car and marching towards Mrs Bannister's gate. All Todd could do was follow her, thoroughly confused. Mandy thumped on the front door. Turning the handle and finding it open, she pushed her way inside. 'Mandy, please!' Todd called helplessly in her wake.

Mandy walked right into Mrs Bannister's low-beamed living room. The old woman was sitting in a flowery armchair with one foot propped up on a stool, turning to stare in wide-eyed bewilderment as first one, then two unexpected visitors suddenly appeared in her home. There was a blanket laid over her legs. A glass of pale sherry on a little table next to her. A soap opera was blaring on the TV. Cats lay everywhere, stretched out on the rug, draped over the back of the sofa and the windowsill. One or two of them looked up lazily at the intruders.

Mandy marched straight over to the television, switched it off and turned to face Mrs Bannister. 'Right, you old bag. Where did you get it? Did Ellen give it to you? Whatever. Just give it back to me. I know what's going on and I've had enough of your bloody games!'

'Mandy—' Todd began.

'You're my witness here,' she snapped at him. 'Just listen, okay?'

'G-give what back?' Mrs Bannister asked, staring wildly at Mandy.

'The key to Summer Cottage. The key you're using to let yourself into my place to try to scare me. What are you doing it for? Why?'

Todd couldn't believe what he was hearing.

'You were there this evening, weren't you?' Mandy raged at the old woman. 'I know it was you I saw at the window. By the time I got back to the cottage, you'd slipped out. And this afternoon, too, sneaking around the bedroom and banging doors downstairs. Just like you were banging on my bedroom door last night. Switching lights on and off like a maniac. I'm warning you. Stay away from me and my house or else—'

'Mandy, please!' Todd yelled.

She turned to him, her face contorted with anger. 'It's true, Todd. I know it's her, even if I didn't get a good look.

Who else could it be? I wouldn't be surprised if she even let that cat in there on purpose, to scare me!'

'But why would she do that?'

'I think I know the answer to that one,' Mandy seethed, turning back to stand threateningly over the old woman, who was shrinking into her armchair. 'She knew Ellen Grace, they were friends and she's got it into her twisted old head that she resents me for being at Summer Cottage. That's right, isn't it? You think you can scare me into leaving. Answer me, you b—'

Mandy broke off mid-word as another woman suddenly appeared from a doorway on the far side of the room. She had shoulder-length fair hair and bore a faint resemblance to Mrs Bannister, but was at least thirty-five years younger.

Todd thought she looked vaguely familiar. Hadn't he seen her somewhere before?

Glowering at the two of them, the woman strode into the room with her fists clenched. 'Who are you to talk to my aunt that way?' she shouted. 'How dare you come bursting in like this? Get out of here!'

'Or what, you'll call the police? Let's do that, shall we?' Mandy retorted furiously. 'They'll know how to deal with a loony old stalker!'

'I am the police,' the woman said.

'Oh, shit,' Todd breathed. Now he remembered where he'd seen the woman before: driving around Fairwood in a patrol car. She looked different out of uniform, with her hair loose.

'WPC Mitchell to you. And if you don't withdraw these accusations and leave right now, you'll be facing much more serious charges yourself.' Stepping over to Mrs Bannister's armchair, the policewoman grasped the blanket draped over her legs and drew it away.

'Jesus,' Mandy groaned, suddenly crestfallen.

Mrs Bannister's lower right leg was enveloped in a thick plaster cast that encased her shin all the way down to the foot resting on the stool. Her wrinkled bare toes stuck pinkly out from the end of the cast.

'She hasn't been anywhere for two days,' said her niece. 'Broken ankle. She can't even get upstairs to her own bed, never mind walk all the way down the lane to your house. I'm off work to look after her, and I've been with her nearly the whole time. So you' – jabbing a finger at Mandy – 'had better put a sock in it before I arrest you for disturbing the peace, threatening behaviour and harassment of a sick, elderly, vulnerable member of the community. Get me?'

It was a painful, mortifying few minutes before Mandy and Todd finally extricated themselves from Mrs Bannister's house and walked back out into the chill air. The night was clearing to give way to a bright, clearly crater-pocked gibbous moon. The silhouetted figure of WPC Mitchell glared at them from the doorway until they were off the property, and then slammed the door.

'Don't say it, Todd, please,' Mandy muttered.

'I tried to stop you,' he said.

'I know you did.'

'What the hell's got into you?'

'Something's happening, Todd. If it wasn't her, then what? You tell me. What?'

Todd's throat was tight with emotion. 'I'm sorry, Mandy, I can't do this any more.'

She saw his expression and looked at him with pleading eyes, brimming with tears. His own eyes were moist.

'I really like you,' he blurted. 'I think I even love you, all right? But we need to be apart until you get yourself sorted out. I'm sorry. I'm just very fucking sorry it had to be like this.'

'Todd!'

'Bye, Mandy,' he said in a strangled voice. And he turned away from her and walked off into the night.

THIRTEEN

MANDY CRIED HERSELF to sleep that night, pulling the bedclothes tightly around her for comfort. She didn't want to be going mad, yet she felt as if her mind was being torn apart. She didn't want to be alone, yet now Todd had left her and she might never see him again.

The moonlight glowed softly through the drawn curtains, growing now dimmer, now brighter as clouds drifted across its face. The cottage seemed alive with a thousand tiny creaks and taps.

Finally asleep with her face pressed to the tear-dampened pillow, Mandy's breathing was slow and steady. It wasn't until the depths of the night that she half-awoke, stiff from lying for hours in the same position, and stirred in the bed. As she moved her leg, her bare foot touched something. The sensation of flesh on flesh woke her with a start. She raised her head from the pillow and twisted round.

'Todd!' she whispered.

He'd come back to her! She drowsily recalled that he'd had the spare key. He must have slipped into bed quietly without wanting wake her. His reassuring presence was right there beside her, the dim moonlight that filtered through the curtain faintly outlining his shape under the covers close by, the strong lines of his back and shoulder. She could hear the softness of his breath.

'Oh, Todd, I'm so happy you came back,' she murmured, gently stroking his shoulder. A rush of tender feeling overcame her and she propped herself up on her left elbow to put her right arm around him, pulling herself close to him.

'I'm so sorry for what happened,' she whispered. I don't know what's got into me. I promise, it won't go on. You mean too much to me. I don't want to lose you.'

He stirred.

'You said you loved me,' she whispered. 'I love you too, Todd.' She caressed his shoulder, his arm, his chest. Pushed herself up so that she could kiss him. Her lips reached for his. It felt so good to be close to him again.

The clouds rolled clear of the moon, so that its light shone more brightly through the curtain.

And Mandy looked down at the thing in the bed with her. A rotted corpse. Green-black skin and rancid worm-eaten flesh peeling from the bone. The leprous eyelids peeled open and the thing's eyes glinted evilly as they looked into hers. Its lipless teeth parted in a grin, the stench of grave-filth and decomposing meat and things that squirmed and feasted on corruption filling her nostrils. She screamed and recoiled, struggling in blind horror to get away, but cadaverous arms encircled her body and held her in a tight clinch. Tighter, tighter, until she could no longer scream, no longer breathe. Its rasping voice cackled in her ear.

Mandyyyyy …

★ ★ ★

'Christ, Mandy. You sound terrible.'

'I had an awful dream last night, Chester. Awful.'

It was morning, and his phone call had interrupted her in the middle of the third, or maybe the fourth, mug of coffee she needed to stay awake. She hadn't stayed in bed after the nightmare, and exhaustion hung over her like a pall.

'No kidding,' said Chester, whose only dreams were of foxy ladies and red Ferraris. 'Anyway, listen, have you gone online this morning? Checked your ebook sales at all?'

'No,' she said miserably.

'Then I suggest you get off your ass and check, girl. I've been glued to 'em since yesterday. You hit the Kindle rankings low, at thirty thousand. To be expected, right? I mean, Jessica Lomax being a complete unknown and all. But then you started to climb, and fast. By nine in the evening you'd hit the Top Hundred. By midnight you were in the Top Fifty. Now you're—'

'What time is it?' she groaned.

'Listen to me,' he hissed. 'You're at number *seven*. Out of over a million titles. Seven. And the reviews are coming in fast. People are loving it! You've sold more in eighteen hours than your last paperback did in a whole eighteen months.'

Despite herself, despite the sickly hangover from the horrible nightmare and the row with Todd, she came away from Chester's phone call feeling a frisson of excitement. As the news sank in, she tried to phone Victoria to tell her, but her friend's mobile was switched off. After that she called Todd's number and left him a short but heartfelt message to say she was terribly sorry and asking him to please, please call her back.

She'd turned on the computer and was about to check the incredible sales ratings herself when she heard the faint ping of an email hitting her inbox.

Not just one email. There were five of them, which for her was extremely unusual. She blinked as she started reading.

> Hi Jessica, I've just got to the end of Orgasm of Blood. Downloaded it at 3 this morning cos I couldn't sleep. Big mistake, now I'll never sleep again!! Love it, scary stuff indeed. Hope there'll be more books to come.
> Charlie

> Loved it. Best horror story Ive read. Your my new fave author!
> Christine

> Hey Jessica,
> I've just finished reading Orgasm of Blood. Really enjoyed it. Was on the edge of my seat from beginning to end. Gave me nightmares, lol.
> Ally

> Hello,
> Quite some time ago, I came across the work of a horror writer called Lucinda Darke. Her style is very similar to yours. Wondered if you'd ever read anything by her? Looking forward to the next book! Keep writing!
> Stacy

> Hi Jessica, I've never written to an author
> before, but after reading Orgasm of Blood, I
> just had to contact you. No writer has creeped
> me out this much since Lucinda Darke. Ever
> since she stopped writing I've been hoping to
> find another author to take her place. You are
> one sick puppy, and I mean that as a sincere
> compliment. ☺
> Pete

Mandy had never heard of any Lucinda Darke, but then she was a stranger to the whole genre. She quickly forgot about the comparisons, closed the email program and went into the Amazon website. Chester's phone announcement was already out of date – *Orgasm of Blood* was number two in the Kindle chart.

Mandy blinked once again. Number Two! And as Chester had said, the positive reviews were piling up. One drew her eye.

> ★ ★ ★ ★ Loved it
> Read it in one sitting. Gave me the creeps
> lol. Don't read ORGASM OF BLOOD if
> you're alone in the house at night. Gave it 4
> stars instead of 5 cos it's a little bit similar to
> Lucinda Darke's NIGHTMARE HOUSE.
> Published 1 day ago by Patsy Pooh

There was that Lucinda Darke again, Mandy thought.

Reading on, she noticed that among the positive comments from readers, a number of highly critical one-star reviews were creeping in. As a writer, she knew that those

were often the handiwork of internet trolls, jealous wan-
nabes, bitter failed authors or friends of the competition.

But these were different.

> ★ Rip Off
> Total waste of time, do not read this
> rubbish. This author is a big copy cat who
> has blatantly ripped off the talent of the far
> superior Lucinda Darke. Don't waste your
> money. One star, only because Amazon
> won't let me give it zero.
> Published today by BookCrazyJo

Book Crazy Jo's review had garnered fifteen comments
from other readers. 'Couldn't agree more!'; 'Absolutely
right!'; 'Plagiarism at its worst'; 'I deleted it off my Kindle
for the same reason'. And on, and on.

'I've never even heard of Lucinda Darke!' Mandy yelled
at the screen. She ran a search for the author's books on
Amazon. There were no Lucinda Darke ebooks, only
paperbacks and a few hardback editions. Five titles in all:
*Nightmare House, The Hidden Room, The Guillotine, Abattoir
Dreams* and *Putrid.* All had been published between 2003
and 2005 by a publisher called Incubus Press. Checking out
the company name on Google, Mandy discovered that it
had been a small press specialising only in horror, based in
Sussex, founded 1979 and closed down in 2008.

Ping. Another email had arrived. Feeling flustered and
agitated, Mandy broke off from her Google search.

Short and to the point, the message was from an
anonymous Hotmail account and read simply:

Jessica Lomax you are a fucking plagiarist.
Shame on you.

'I've had enough of this shit,' Mandy muttered. She might be slowly losing her mind, but she was no plagiarist. Something had to be done about the situation, but first she had to check out these Lucinda Darke books to determine what these allegations were based on.

It was already after eleven. Mandy piled Buster in the Kia and headed into Fairwood. The village library was only open two days a week and had limited stock: none of the Darke titles were listed there. On further investigation, though, the kindly man behind the desk was able to find out that the public library in Burford had three of the books.

Burford was the largest town in the area, twelve miles away. What the hell, Mandy thought, and sped out of Fairwood with grim determination.

It was forty minutes later when she walked into Burford library. Heading straight for the fiction section she found *Putrid, Abattoir Dreams* and *The Guillotine* under D for Darke. She slid the yellowed paperbacks off the shelf and took them to a secluded reading table for a closer look.

The covers were as morbid and lurid as anything she could imagine, and worse. Skimming through the pages she soon saw that the horror element in Lucinda Darke's writing was powerful and compulsive, drawing the reader in with suspenseful skill while turning their stomachs with grotesque scenes of torture, mutilation, necrophilia, cannibalism and ritual child sacrifice.

What also struck her was the writer's particularly distinctive voice. There was something strangely familiar about it: the authorly quirks, the mannerisms, the favourite expressions and turns of phrase.

As if … as if she'd read this writer's work before.

As if she'd known it. Known it for years, only under another name.

It slowly began to dawn on Mandy what she was seeing here on these yellowed, well-thumbed pages.

Could it be possible? The very thought chilled her. She *had* to know, and the only way to do that was to read more. Clutching the books under her arm, she went to the main desk and asked the lady librarian if any more titles by this author were in stock. The librarian disappeared for a moment, then returned holding a large-format hardback, explaining it had been returned earlier in the day and not yet found its way back to the shelves.

The book was Lucinda Dark's *Nightmare House*. Mandy carried it back to her table and tore into it with an uneasy mixture of revulsion and eagerness. Halfway down page eighteen, she came to a passage that made her shiver. She went back and read it carefully a second time to make sure she hadn't imagined it.

It was a description of a house. More correctly, of a cottage. One with a thatched roof. An old oak front door with a cast-iron lion's head for a lock. Inside, a carved fireplace that featured a heraldic beast of some kind, gargoyle-like in its fierceness.

There was no mistaking Summer Cottage, right there on the page. Except that from the pen of Lucinda Darke it was horrifyingly sinister, evoking a tone of malevolence that Mandy could hardly bear to take in. Her mouth became dry as she read on, unable to take her eyes from the faded print.

Valerie crept down the twisted passageway
towards the light that was emanating from the
cellar. It beckoned to her. It spoke to her.

Valerieeee …

Valerieeee …

Enticing her to go down the steps. Inviting
her. Luring her.

And Valerie could not refuse. Like a
sleepwalker she stepped into the light and was
swallowed by it.

Mandy's hands had begun to shake so badly that the pages
were fluttering. She slammed the book shut. 'No,' she
groaned, hanging her head. 'It can't be. It's a coincidence.'
All her strength seemed to have drained away. The book
flopped open in her limp hand, and she saw the author's
signature on the title page.

Lucinda Darke. The curve of the 'a' and the 'r'. The
upturned flick of the 'l' and the tail of the 'e'.

No mistake.

She'd seen that handwriting before. Coveted it. Idolised it.
It was the handwriting of Ellen Grace.

She was barely conscious of checking the pile of books
out of the library and walking back to the car, just as she'd
been barely conscious of time passing while she'd been
inside. Darkness was falling again, and the mist that had
seemed to haunt the village of Fairwood the day before
had now descended over Burford. The windows of the Kia
were steamed up with condensation from the dog's breath.
Mandy slumped behind the wheel, laid the books beside

her in their carrier bag on the passenger seat and drove away feeling numb.

She understood now. Knew it deep inside.

Lucinda Darke. Ellen Grace. One and the same.

The horror novels had all been written between 2002 and 2005: the same years Ellen had spent at Summer Cottage. Everyone thought she'd only written one book during her time there. The truth was very different. Ellen Grace had been busy. Busy prolifically churning out thousands of pages of gruesome, morbid horror, not because she wanted to, not out of choice.

But because her writer's imagination had unwittingly, irresistibly, become the channel for something unspeakable that she couldn't control or understand, any more than Mandy had been able to.

A force that had possessed her. Taken over her mind with nightmarish visions. Sapped her vitality, robbed her of her sanity, turned her into a withered recluse.

Something terrible existed at Summer Cottage.

And now it had a new victim.

FOURTEEN

'I'M SORRY, MIKE. I really am. There's just no way I can make it down there.'

'It's a damn shame, Todd, but I understand. You do sound pretty rough. You know what's good for the flu? Hot whisky, lots of honey in it, and lemon juice. Come to think of it, probably doesn't do much real good, but the whisky perks you up a bit.'

'I'll give it a try.'

'You do that, mate. Take it easy, okay?'

'Thanks, Mike,' Todd said, and hung up the phone. He felt bad about letting down his client, even worse for lying to the guy. Mike's small advertising agency in Cornwall had given him a lot of business over the years, and now he was leaving them in the lurch to find someone else at very short notice.

But nothing could be done about it, Todd thought. He was just too damned upset to focus on anything right now. He didn't want to be around people. Only her.

Mandy. Mandy. He kept thinking of her. Couldn't tear his thoughts away, not for a second. All he could do was mope about the house, trying to think of what to say to her, wondering when he'd see her again, wishing they hadn't fought, wishing he hadn't run off like that.

He had to talk to her. Had to see her.

Grabbing his car keys and shrugging on his jacket, he closed his front door and walked the few yards down the quiet, amber-lit village street to where he'd parked the Volvo. It was dark, and getting misty again. He got into the car and twisted the key in the ignition.

Nothing. Dead battery. He swore and thumped the steering wheel in frustration. This wasn't going to stop him. It was only half a mile from the edge of Fairwood to Summer Cottage. He'd walk it.

By the time he reached the lane leading to her house, the mist had thickened so much that someone unsure of their bearings would easily have got lost out here. Approaching the gate he saw through the trees that the place was all in darkness. Her car wasn't there, either. He wondered where she'd gone. Hoped she was all right.

Now he wasn't sure what to do. Should he just go home, maybe pay a visit to the pub and drown his sorrows in beer? Or he could hang about here until she returned, but it could be hours. That was when he remembered the key in his pocket. He felt for it, closed his fingers on the rough black iron and pulled it out.

Okay, he thought, what I need to do is let myself in, write her a note to tell her I'm sorry I said those things and that I want to see her again really soon. When she comes back from wherever she's gone, maybe she'll call me.

He turned the key in the lion's-head lock and the door swung open, gaping wide to invite him into the blackness of the entrance hall. He stepped inside and groped for the light switch. The lights flickered on, faded for a moment and then flickered back on. Bad connection somewhere, he thought. He'd investigate the problem, but not now.

He wiped his muddy feet on the mat, then walked up the passage to Mandy's writing study, knowing he'd find some paper there on which to write a note. Taking a sheet of A4 from the fresh sheaf in the printer and a pen from the little jar on her desk, he paused to think of the best way to express his feelings. This could sound so lame if he didn't get it right.

It was while he paused that he heard the giggle. He turned to look out of the study doorway. It had come from further down the passage.

'Mandy?' he called out.

There it was again. Laughter, female laughter, soft but perfectly distinct.

He replaced the pen in the jar and loaded the blank paper back into the printer, then left the study and headed down the passage in the direction of the sound. He passed the dining room door on his left, then the kitchen door. Both rooms were dark.

'Mandy?' he called again. He halted a moment to flick on one of the Bakelite switches he admired so much. Another light came on, illuminating the empty passage ahead for just an instant or two before it flickered, died, came dimly back on again. Definitely something wrong with the electrics, he decided. So much for the period charm of old houses.

He'd gone a few more yards down the passage when the lights died altogether. Plunged into darkness, he stopped. 'Well, we saw that coming,' he muttered. Didn't Mandy keep a torch somewhere? Yes, but he'd never find it.

He stumbled on, feeling his way. Found another switch and waggled it. Nope. Dead. Mandy must be somewhere at the back of the house, the utility room or the laundry room, probably hunting about looking for a torch or a candle to light. He hoped he wouldn't scare her half to death, appearing in the dark in the middle of a bloody power cut. 'Mandy,' he called in a strong voice, to alert her of his presence. 'It's me, Todd. Where are you?'

When he saw the glimmering glow up ahead his first thought was that she must have lit a candle. It wasn't, though. It was almost like some kind of floating, strangely phosphorescent mist that grew inexplicably thicker as he made his way deeper into the passage. The peculiar, sickly greenish-yellow light seemed to be more intense further along, beyond the point where the passage curved out of sight.

He called her name again.

This time, as if in reply, came another sound. It wasn't the female laughter he'd heard before. It was a snickering cackle. It wasn't far away.

Todd felt his flesh turn a little colder. 'Stop messing around, Mandy,' he called out, and heard the nervous tremor in his own voice.

He followed the bend in the passage, the strange, intensifying glow ahead somehow leading him on. Through it, he saw a door. He remembered what Mandy had told him and the chill in his body became a shudder.

So the cottage had a cellar, after all. He'd been so willing to disbelieve her; scepticism was a luxury he no longer possessed.

He was suddenly terribly afraid. Gripped by a panicked desire to turn and run, he realised that he couldn't. He was being drawn to the cellar door.

Now he was standing at its threshold. He reached out with a quaking hand, but before he could touch it the door swung open, and he found himself looking down a twisting stone stairway.

Something like cobwebs brushed his face. The eerie light shone intensely from down there. Unable to stop himself, he began to head downwards into the cellar. His footsteps echoed off the craggy stone walls that surrounded him.

The door closed behind him with a reverberating thud.

And when he saw what was coming towards him from below, his mouth opened for a scream that never found voice.

FIFTEEN

AFTER GETTING CAUGHT up in traffic jams on the A40, Mandy didn't get back to Summer Cottage until early evening. She shivered as she opened the front door, feeling a chill there that she was certain wasn't just caused by the dropping outside temperature or the mist that hung heavy in the night air. When she flipped on the lights, they seemed to flicker uncertainly before coming on.

Buster was plainly unhappy to leave the car and she had to coax him into the cottage with a dog treat. He made for his bed in the kitchen, and sat there looking tense. Mandy stayed near him for a while, fretting, then walked uneasily into the hallway and picked up the phone to dial Sarah Grace's number.

'Don't hesitate to call,' Ellen's daughter had said in her note. Now was the time to find out some truths. *What really happened to your mother?* Mandy wanted to ask. *Did she ever report anything strange about this house?*

Another question had begun to plague her, too. When she'd first seen the asking price Sarah Grace had put on her mother's former home, Mandy had been too bowled over by her good fortune to think twice about it. Even after seeing the place, she hadn't questioned why someone in her position on the property ladder could possibly afford it. But now she wondered. Why had Sarah Grace sold Summer Cottage so cheap? Did she know something?

But Mandy hung up the phone before she'd even finished dialling. How could she ask those things without being taken for a lunatic? And if Sarah did know anything, she was hardly likely to admit it to her.

She did need help, though, and fast. She ran to the study, glancing nervously up and down the passage. Her skin crawled with the feeling that, everywhere she went in the house, she was being watched. She quickly turned on the computer, brought up the Google search box and keyed in the words 'paranormal investigator cotswolds'. She hit Enter. The search results flashed up, showing only one name. A few clicks later, Mandy was looking at the website of one Claire Baker, based not too far away in Stow on the Wold and offering services to clients who believed they were being affected by "phenomena that seem to defy rational explanation". Ms Baker claimed several years' experience in investigating hauntings and other paranormal activity across south and central England. Her photo showed a benevolent-looking woman in her late forties or early fifties, with short reddish hair and the puffy face of someone with a long-term weight problem.

Mandy hastily scribbled down the woman's phone number. Email wasn't quick enough for what she had in mind.

The feeling in the house was getting stronger. As if the unseen watchers were everywhere, circling her, moving in closer with each passing moment. She couldn't bear it any more. 'Come on, Buster,' she called, throwing open the kitchen door. 'We're going.'

She locked the cottage and ran back to the car with the dog at her heels, dived into the Kia and sped away, fog-lights cutting twin swathes through the ponderous mist. She drove for miles further out into the countryside, putting distance between her and Summer Cottage. The feeling of relief for having got away from the place should have been immense, but she couldn't escape the sense of dread that seemed to hang on her, on her clothes, her hair, like a putrid stink.

The layby she pulled up in was off a deserted country road. She reached into her bag for her mobile phone, little used since moving to Summer Cottage and somehow a comforting reminder of her life before coming to this place. In the darkness of the car she pressed Claire Baker's number into the tiny glowing keys and made the call.

Dial tone.

Please, please, don't be a fruitcake or a whacko. Please be what I need.

'Hello?' said a woman's voice on the line. So far, she sounded normal.

'Is that Claire Baker?'

'Speaking.'

'I'm sorry to bother you in the evening,' Mandy said. She spoke in a hushed tone, unable to shake the feeling that other listeners could hear her. 'Oh, Christ. I don't know how to say this.'

'Why don't you just come straight out with it, dear?' The woman spoke slowly. Her voice sounded warm and comforting.

'I'll try. There's ... there's something in my house. Something bad. Something ...' Mandy swallowed. 'Evil. It's after me. I think it wants to hurt me.' She broke into a sob.

'Relax. What's your name?'

'Mandy.'

'Relax, Mandy. Do you believe you're in danger?'

Mandy sniffed. 'Yes. Yes, I do.'

'Is the danger present at this very moment?'

Mandy glanced around her. Shadows from the waving trees outside played against the car windows. The mist drifted by. Buster was whingeing quietly in the back seat. 'No. I'm not at the house now. I'm safe. I think.'

'Then calm down and tell me your problem, in your own words.'

Over the next couple of minutes Mandy gave a halting, broken account of the events since her arrival at Summer Cottage. 'Please help me. I didn't know who else to call.'

'You did the right thing, dear.' Claire Baker's voice was warm and soft. 'Let me tell you that virtually all of the phenomena attributed to the paranormal turn out to have a perfectly rational explanation. A large part of the work investigators like myself carry out is to help soothe the anxiety that comes with the false belief that we're dealing with some harmful or malevolent power.'

'That's what I so want to believe,' Mandy told her. 'That I'm just imagining the whole thing. That life can be normal again. Otherwise I just don't know what I'm going to do.' Her voice was near cracking.

A pause on the line. 'Did you say Fairwood? That's not far for me to travel. I could come out to you tomorrow morning, say ten-thirty?'

Mandy felt her heart sink. The idea of waiting that long was unthinkable. 'Please, I'm desperate. Couldn't you come now?'

'Now?'

'This evening, as soon as possible. I'm begging you. I'll pay you double your normal rate. Name a price.'

A longer pause. Then: 'That won't be necessary. Give me your address, dear. I'll get there as soon as I can.'

Slowly and with a sense of apprehension that grew stronger with every mile, Mandy drove back towards Summer Cottage. When the dark shape of the house loomed through the trees she pulled up within sight of it, no closer. And waited.

After half an hour she was beginning to think Claire Baker wouldn't show; then headlights glowed on the lane and a car trundled slowly past the property, as if searching for an address. It stopped. The driver's door opened and as the car's inside light came on, Mandy recognised the woman from her website photo.

Mandy emerged from the parked Kia, clutching the carrier bag containing the library books, and stepped out into the cold mist to greet her. 'Thank you so much for coming, Ms Baker,' she said with real gratitude as they shook hands.

'Please, call me Claire. You sounded as if you were serious about needing help. I notice—'

'That I waited in the car for you to arrive?' Mandy nodded. 'I can't be in there alone.'

'Well, you're not alone now, dear,' Claire said with a warm smile, and took her arm. 'Shall we go inside? Let's talk about it over a nice cup of tea.'

'So how does this work?' Mandy asked nervously as they entered the cottage. Noticing that all the investigator had brought with her was a small, slim briefcase, she asked, 'Don't you use – I don't know – special equipment or something?'

'Sometimes,' Claire said. 'Cameras triggered by movement, sensors to pick up sudden temperature drops, electromagnetic frequency meters, things like that. But I don't tend to use them as much as some others in my line of work. I rely a lot on instinct, but that's just my personal preference.'

'By instinct, you mean, psychic ability?'

Claire smiled. 'Oh, I wouldn't make any great claim to special powers. But I have a *lot* of instinct.' She gazed around her for a moment at the hallway, as if drinking in the atmosphere of Summer Cottage. No expression showed on her face. 'Now, wherever's most comfortable for you to sit down and talk—'

'The kitchen,' Mandy said, with a nervous glance up the passage.

'Then let's go into the kitchen,' Claire said in that calm, patient manner.

The investigator was very professional, very organised. From her briefcase she produced a notebook and a paranormal incident report form, on which she quickly filled out Mandy's name and address together with the date. Her hands were chubby, with red nails. Taking out a small digital voice recorder she asked if she could record their interview. 'Good. Let's begin.' She turned on the recorder.

As they talked, her questions were deliberately open, letting Mandy tell her story, never leading her. Mandy could tell she was being discreetly assessed to ensure she wasn't a fraud or hoaxster. Claire must get a lot of those, she thought.

The investigator made notes as Mandy talked. 'Would it be possible for me to speak with Todd? I'd like to get his side of the situation.'

'Todd doesn't believe me. Thinks I'm going mad, or that I've burned myself out working too hard.'

'I see. Now, you say you're a writer. What is it you write about?'

'Well, normally I write historical romance novels.' Hesitantly at first, Mandy explained how all that had changed soon after she'd come to live here. 'I've never experienced anything like it before, or had such ideas. It's frightening how clear they were. Still are. And now I've discovered that the author who lived here before me – the *same thing happened to her.* She wrote these.' Mandy opened up the carrier bag she'd brought from the car, and showed Claire the Lucinda Darke books. 'That was just another name Ellen wrote under,' she explained.

Claire spent a few moments examining the books. If she was shocked by the covers or the content, she didn't show it. She laid them aside, was quiet for a moment and then said, 'You mentioned this neighbour—'

'Mrs Bannister.'

'Perhaps I could talk to her, too? It's important for me to gather as much information as possible, from all sources and angles.'

Mandy gave a sour laugh. 'I don't think that's a good idea. I've already been warned to stay away. One false move and I'll be arrested by her copper niece.'

'Very well,' Claire said, signalling the end of the interview. She reached for her briefcase and replaced everything back inside, apart from the digital sound recorder which Mandy noticed she slipped into her pocket.

'That's it?' Mandy said.

Claire smiled. 'More or less, for now. I'd just like to take a few minutes to walk about the house alone, if I may. Just to gain my own impressions.'

'Then you'll excuse me if I wait outside.'

'Of course, dear.'

Mandy returned to the car, feeling somewhat deflated and quite unsure what to make of the interview. She'd expected more, somehow. She sat in the Kia with Buster for nearly twenty minutes before she saw the paranormal investigator emerge from Summer Cottage. Claire walked calmly to Mandy's car.

'Well?' Mandy said, trying to gauge the woman's expression. Nothing seemed to be wrong. Was that a good thing?

'That's it,' Claire said. 'Thank you, dear, you've been very helpful.'

'And now what?'

'Now I go back and reflect on my notes, assess the case and decide whether to investigate further.'

'But I thought you'd agreed—'

Claire held up a hand. 'Please be patient. I know it's not easy.'

'But what do I do if you don't take the case on and—'

'Try and remain calm. Do you have another place to go, if you prefer to stay away from home for now?'

'I can find a place,' Mandy said.

'That's good. I'll be in touch. Good night, dear.'

And with that, Claire Baker walked back to her car, leaving Mandy very much alone again. Mandy watched her drive away. She obviously thinks I'm crazy, she thought. Maybe the woman was just a crank, after all.

Whatever the case, there was no way Mandy was going

to sleep at Summer Cottage that night. 'Let's get out of here, Buster,' she muttered disconsolately as she started the Kia.

There was a cosy inn in the village, but they had no rooms vacant. Next, Mandy tried a bed and breakfast she'd noticed near the solicitors' offices, but was turned away by the surly woman there on the grounds that they didn't allow pets.

'Please, I can't leave him in the car alone. He'll pine.'

'Not my problem.' The woman closed the door in her face.

She tried calling Todd's number. There was no answer, so she drove to his terraced house a little way from the pub on Main Street and rang the doorbell. He wasn't there. *Of course he wasn't*, she realised with a sinking feeling as she remembered him mentioning that upcoming job in Cornwall.

But as she was returning to her car, she noticed the Volvo estate a few yards down the street. Surely he wouldn't have gone off by train to a photo shoot, she thought. Not with all that gear he had to lug about with him. Peering through the grimy back window of the estate, she could see the aluminium boxes piled up inside by the glow of the streetlight.

Then maybe he hadn't gone to Cornwall after all! The job could have fallen through at the last minute. With a flash of hope, it occurred to her that she might find him at his favourite hangout, the nearby Fox and Hounds.

After making sure that Buster was safely locked inside the Kia, she ran down the street and burst inside the warm, lively pub. A young couple sat at the table nearest the fire where Todd liked to sit. Mandy went to the bar and asked the barman if Todd had been in that night. 'Not seen him since yesterday,' was the reply.

She walked back to the Kia, feeling lonely and frightened as it dawned on her that there was nothing for it but to spend the night in the car. 'Looks like it's just you and me, boy,' she said to Buster.

Mandy drove and drove, trying to get as far away as possible from what had once been her ideal home. When the emotions became too strong for her to carry on driving, she pulled over in the leafy, whispering shadows of a rural picnic area and fell sobbing against the steering wheel.

'Oh, Todd, where are you?'

SIXTEEN

CLAIRE BAKER DROVE back to Stow on the Wold much faster than she normally would, with her hands tightly clutching the wheel and her brows knitted in deep thought. Reaching the boxy, detached modern house on the edge of Stow that she'd shared with her husband Dave before his death seven years earlier, she parked the car in the leaf-strewn drive, grabbed her coat and briefcase and hurried to the front door.

She was sweating, edgy with the same profound sense of unease that had come over her from the very first moment she'd walked inside the home of her new client. It had been a terrible struggle to contain herself, to maintain an outward appearance of professional composure as the awful fear had steadily grown throughout the interview – and with it the overwhelming urge to pack up her things and run, and keep running.

When the interview had ended and she'd faced the task of exploring the property alone to confirm what she already dreaded, the fear had become amplified to near-crippling terror. That solitary walk through the rooms and passageways of Summer Cottage had taken everything she'd got, and left her literally breathless from a sensation of pervading malevolence that seemed to ooze from every crack and crevice of that old house – and still clung to her now.

Claire had never regarded herself as anything more than a moderately receptive psychic. A few times in her life, before becoming a paranormal investigator and since, she'd picked up on atmospheres, auras, energies, whatever one wished to call these things her limited talent allowed her to perceive. Never before had she sensed anything as horrifyingly powerful as the ambiance at Summer Cottage, or even imagined she could. And she never wanted to feel anything like it again.

With the front door locked behind her, she dropped her coat and briefcase on the sitting room floor and headed straight for the kitchen to pour herself a large gin. Knocking it down in nervous gulps, she went through into the spare downstairs bedroom she used as an office. The digital sound recorder was still in her pocket. She set it on the desk, turned it back on and replayed the recording of the interview with her client Mandy Freeman. She paced the room and sipped her gin as she listened, concentrating hard on every word of Mandy's account and her replies to the questions Claire had asked her.

Now came the bit Claire most dreaded. What she hadn't informed her client of was that she'd intended to keep the sound recorder running during her solitary twenty-minute post-interview exploration of Summer Cottage.

Hearing it again relayed in high-quality digital playback made her blood chill. The sound of her hesitant footsteps. Every creak of an opening door. Every groan and crack of a loose floorboard. Now and then, she could hear the raspy flutter of her own breathing, the occasional groan as she fought to contain her terror.

And something else picked up by the sensitive microphone. It was just the tiniest of background sounds, but it plunged Claire straight back into the moment and made the glass of gin tremble in her fingers. It was what she'd hoped she'd only imagined. Now she knew it had been real.

A low, snickering cackle. Then a guttural voice, barely audible. The words it spoke, even the tongue in which they were uttered, weren't clear. But its intentions were. Oh, so clear.

Reeling, she had to steady herself against the desk. 'Oh, God,' she moaned. She pressed her hand to her heart until the sharp twinge of pain had passed.

Now she knew what she had to do. There was something here that lay far beyond her own skills as a paranormal investigator. She wouldn't be able to help her client.

But if anyone could, it was Tabitha Lake.

Claire soon found the number in the address book. Taking deep breaths to steady her voice, she dialled, waited. Then frowned as the answerphone kicked in and a record-ed message informed her that the Director of the Lake Institute was currently out of the country on a lecture tour and wouldn't be back for three more weeks.

Damn. Claire held on for the beep, then left her message.

'Tabitha, it's Claire Baker. You probably won't remember me, but I took one of your courses a few years ago. You always told me that, if I ever had a problem, to phone you. Well, I do have a problem, one that I'm simply not qualified or able to deal with on my own.'

She paused, fighting to control the panic in her voice. 'You see, I have a client whom I believe to be in terrible danger from an entity in her home, far more than even she realises. I feel I should warn her to stay away from there and never return, but I don't know whether it's ethical for me to recommend such extreme measures to a client. What I do know for certain is that I'm completely out of my depth dealing with something as powerful as this. I'm really frightened, Tabitha. Please, please get in touch as soon as you can.'

After giving her number, Claire hung up and let out a sigh of bitter disappointment. What if Tabitha Lake didn't call back for three weeks? She couldn't wait that long.

Pouring herself another stiff gin, she debated the issue and became more convinced than ever that she'd done the wrong thing by hiding her intuitions from Mandy Freeman. Surely she had to be warned never to set foot in that awful house ever again, even if it meant coming away with nothing but the clothes she wore? The idea of telling that poor young woman to leave her own home was unthinkable. But better that than …

Claire closed her eyes, shuddering.

Mandy had said she wouldn't return to Summer Cottage that night. That meant that she was safe, at least for the moment.

'I'll call her in the morning,' Claire said out loud. 'That's all I can do.'

Suddenly exhausted, she switched off the downstairs lights and dragged herself up the thickly carpeted stairs. A relaxing bath might soothe the tension in her muscles before going to bed, she thought. Reaching the galleried landing, she walked into her bathroom and went over to run the bath. She closed the bathroom door to keep the heat in, went to the bedroom to fetch a fresh towel from the cupboard—

And thought, 'No, bloody hell. Tomorrow morning's not good enough. I've got to call Mandy right now. Tell her to stay away from that place, no matter what.'

She turned to head back downstairs. She was halfway down when she heard the sound, and froze.

The loud banging at the front door seemed to echo around the whole house. Startled at first, Claire suddenly remembered what season it was. Halloween seemed to come around sooner every year these days and with it the intrusive Trick or Treat antics of the local kids.

But as she stood there looking down, the banging resumed so violently that it seemed it might knock the door in. This wasn't kids playing about. Possibilities flew through her mind as she cringed on the stairs. A burglar? The police? She'd heard of drug raids accidentally getting the wrong address.

Something deep in her mind told her it was neither. And the terror of that realisation made her knees wobble under her.

There was a juddering crash as the front door flew off its hinges with such force that it ripped down the inner door leading through to the sitting room. Smashed fragments of splintered wood and door-frame and plasterwork exploded into the house, together with a storm of autumn leaves that billowed and swirled as if caught in the vortex of a gale. A roaring filled Claire's ears as the storm ripped at her hair and clothes. She screamed and ran panic-stricken up the stairs to escape, reached the landing and staggered towards her open bedroom door.

The door swung shut in her face, pushed by an unseen force. She screamed again. The bathroom door was just to her right. Her flailing hand clutched the handle and she burst in, slipping on the shiny floor tiles and almost falling headlong. She kicked the door shut behind her and threw herself against it, groping for the bolt and feeling it slide home. Her breath was coming in heaving gasps and her heart was pounding dangerously as she backed away from the locked door, staring at it, fully expecting it to come crashing in, blown off its hinges by what was out there.

All was silent for a few instants, no sound but the rasp of her lungs and the rush of water from the bath taps. Steam was billowing up and turning the mirror tiles around the bath opaque with condensation.

She sensed a movement. Something was behind her. She whirled around, but she never saw the thing that seized hold of her and dashed her with inhuman force to the floor, face first. She felt the teeth break in her mouth, tasted the blood that welled down her throat. Half stunned, she felt something grip her ankle, felt herself being dragged across the bathroom. Towards the bath itself. She shrieked as brutally strong fingers twisted themselves into her hair, jerked her up as if she weighed nothing and thrust her face towards the billowing steam rising from the bathwater.

The last thing she saw before her head was plunged under was that the water was boiling. *Literally* boiling, its surface bubbling like a cauldron over a fire. Her mouth opened to scream: NOOOOO! Then her cry became a tortured burbling as the thing forced her head and shoulders into the boiling water and held her there. Scalding liquid filled her eyes, her ears, her nose, the agony almost stopping her heart.

Almost, but not quite. She was still alive as the thing jerked her head back out of the blood-clouded water. She caught a glimpse of her steamy reflection in the mirror tiles, her face blistered and cooked crimson by the heat.

The entity drove her face into the tiles with a crunch of flesh and bone against splintering glass. Now Claire Baker couldn't see a thing any longer.

By the time her brains had been beaten out against the edge of the bath, she was already dead.

SEVENTEEN

UNABLE TO SLEEP for the terrors in her head, Mandy went on driving through the night. If she had an aim, it was just to get away, to put as many miles between herself and Summer Cottage as she could. She wanted never to return.

The mist had become a thick fog, forcing her to slow down to a crawl in places and lean forward in the driver's seat, squinting in concentration through the windscreen. Several times she almost drove right into the verge or hit a tree. She'd completely lost her bearings, unsure even what road she was on. How long had she been driving, she wondered in bewilderment. Surely she'd have to come to a village or town sooner or later? Somewhere she could stop and rest, buy a cup of coffee, maybe even find a room. She yearned so badly for a safe haven that she could have wept.

'It won't be long, now, Buster, I promise.' He'd hardly stopped whining in agitation the whole time they'd been driving, which only served to increase her own rising tension.

As the Kia advanced slowly down yet another narrow country lane, Mandy thought she could see houses up ahead. Thank God!

No, it was just one house, she thought, peering through the thick mist. Her eyes were getting strained and hard to focus. Taking a hand off the steering wheel she rubbed one eye, then the other, and looked again.

She stamped on the brake and the car slithered to a halt on the wet road.

'Oh, no, no! It can't be!'

But it was. She was back at Summer Cottage.

Mandy revved the engine hard and threw the car around to go speeding off blindly through the fog in the direction she'd come. 'Buster, quiet!' she yelled. He seemed to have gone out of his mind with fear, barking and growling at nothing. As if visibility weren't already bad enough, he was getting the windows all steamed up with his frantic panting. Mandy rubbed a hole in the condensation on her windscreen and sped onwards, just managing to keep the swerving car on the road.

She came to a turning. Which way: left or right? Did it matter, as long as she was getting further from that place? She turned left, accelerating quickly off. The road snaked onwards for two, three miles, then another junction appeared ahead and this time she took the right turning. On, and on; and in all this time she still hadn't seen another vehicle, or come to a major road, let alone a town. 'This can't be possible!' she yelled, slapping the wheel.

As if in reply, the fog ahead seemed to roll in even more thickly, so that the glare of the Kia's headlamps just reflected back at her, dazzling her and forcing her to slow down even more.

Then out of the mist, the familiar shape loomed up yet again.

No matter which way she turned, no matter how far she went, she couldn't escape from it.

Summer Cottage.

In her shock, Mandy slammed her foot down on the wrong pedal and the car accelerated with a jolt, engine speeding. Before she could get the vehicle under control, a green wall of foliage came racing towards her windscreen. The car's suspension juddered as the wheels hit the verge; then the Kia ploughed into the bushes. Mandy felt herself thrown forward against the pressure of the seatbelt. There was a loud crunch and the windscreen suddenly burst inwards.

Then, nothing. Just the tick of hot metal and the spinning of a rear wheel where the back of the crashed car was raised off the ploughed-up verge. Mandy struggled upright and saw the black, wetly glistening tree branch that had punched through the windscreen and between the front seats, showering the inside of the car with glass fragments. Eight inches further to the right, and it would have impaled her where she sat.

Her second thought was for the dog, who'd been thrown forward under the impact and was lying dazed on the floor of the car. 'Buster! Are you okay?'

Even before she'd said it, Buster was back on his feet and going wild again with frenzied barking. And before Mandy could grab his collar, he'd bounded between the front seats, his paws raking broken glass, then bounced up onto the buckled dashboard and threw himself out through the jagged hole in the windscreen. He went sliding down the crumpled bonnet and disappeared. Mandy heard his frantic barking as he ran off.

'Buster! Come back!'

She twisted herself around in the driver's seat and kicked against her door, which opened with a scrape of twigs and branches. As she clambered out into the mist she saw Buster's distinct white shape pelting across the road.

Heading like a thing possessed towards Summer Cottage. Growling and snarling, the dog scrambled under the gate and ran up the path towards the front door. Running after him, shouting 'Buster! Stop!', Mandy saw the front door suddenly glide open. Buster disappeared into the shadows of the entrance.

'No! Come back!' she yelled, bursting through the gate. Now she couldn't see him at all. She sprinted up the path and in through the open doorway.

Inside Summer Cottage.

EIGHTEEN

MANDY FELT THE chill drape over her like a cold, wet blanket as she stepped inside the hallway. She hardly dared to raise her voice to call Buster's name. From somewhere up the passage she could hear his demented growling and the scratch of his little claws on the stone floor. She tried the lights. The inky darkness remained.

Buster's distant growling suddenly became a furious barking. Then an agonised squealing that quickly dropped away to flat silence.

'Buster!' Mandy wailed. She ran through the blackness of the hall and down the passage, depending almost completely on feel and her knowledge of the place. The dark was all-enveloping, no longer like empty space but somehow imbued with its own material substance that seemed to caress her, lick her, as she forced her way blindly deeper into the house.

But now a glowing light, just a hint at first, enough photons to register the faintest impression on the human eye, seemed to drift and dance up ahead. And now it was growing brighter, a greenish-yellow haze that cast shadows through the twisting angles of the passage. It was the light from her nightmares. The light that Ellen Grace had described through the pen of her pseudonym Lucinda Darke.

And Mandy was stumbling towards it, drawn to its source as if mesmerised. The passage led her on, and on.

And now Mandy found herself approaching the door. It opened for her as she stepped closer. The luminous green mist swirling and curling itself around her, luring her down steps leading steeply beneath the house. She followed them downwards, one by one. Behind her, the door closed with an echo that filled the narrow arched stone tunnel in which she now found herself.

Down and down she went. She lost count of the number of steps she descended, until it seemed as if the steep arched shaft had taken her miles inside the earth. Was she dreaming? Hallucinating, or in some trance? The greenish-yellow light flickered like cold fire up ahead, more intense than ever, outlining the craggy arch of the tunnel. A few steps later she felt a cold breeze through her hair and realised numbly that she'd reached the end of the tunnel.

In front of her, the narrow space opened up into a greenly illuminated cavern whose vastness was too incredible for her brain to take in. Beyond the reaches of the light it stretched out into ethereal darkness that might have been infinite.

Mandy staggered on through the misty light. Strange voices seemed to echo through the cavern, snickerings and chortlings that made her whirl round this way and then that. The voices seemed to tease her, enjoying her terror. The air was pungent with the marshlike stench of the slimy things that emerged from the ground around her as she walked. The patter and squeal of rats was everywhere; other unseen creatures seemed to scuttle and slither away from her approach. She could feel the many eyes watching her from the darkness.

She was beyond terror now, beyond rational thought, into a realm that had stretched her mind past the point of ever returning. Tears ran down her face, dripped off her chin, tasted salty on her lips. The ground squelched under her feet, making it hard to walk.

She stumbled and fell with a cry, landing on outstretched hands, the weight of her body making her fingers sink into the softness that had broken her fall. Too late, the rank stench reached her nostrils and she recoiled, scrabbling backwards in the filth with a cry of disgust. Looking at her hands, the rotted flesh and blood dripping from her fingers. Gaping down at the half-eaten, ripped and mutilated corpse at her feet. Todd's eyes stared up into hers but saw nothing.

Mandy's scream reverberated around the cavern. And from the darkness came the laughter of unseen things too terrible even for nightmares.

She staggered away, weeping, gibbering, on the brink of madness, until her legs buckled under her and she collapsed on her face.

And from between her hands plunged deep into the ooze, a half-buried skull grinned at her. A few wisps of platinum blond hair still hung limp from the cracked bone. Tatters of blackened skin were all the rats had left attached to the rest of the skeleton.

Mandy moaned and tried to struggle upright, but there was nothing solid underfoot and nothing she could do to stop herself slipping back down into the rotting slime.

Her fingers closed on some small, hard object. With a wet sucking sound she drew it from the putrescence and held it up in the light.

The little chain dangled from her fingers, dripping filth. The part of Mandy's mind that was still capable of sane thought recognised the thing in her hand. It was the cameo pendant that had once belonged to Ellen Grace.

The blond-haired skull leered up at her. Cackles of knowing laughter echoed around the cavern.

Because *they* knew that Mandy Freeman wouldn't leave this place. She was trapped down here. Face to face with her favourite writer.

EPILOGUE

Excerpt from the *Oxford Times*

Six months on, Thames Valley Police are still examining leads in the search for Ms Mandy Freeman, author of several historical romance novels. Shortly prior to her disappearance last October, Ms Freeman, 32, had moved to the Fairwood home of the international best-selling writer Ellen Grace, who herself vanished under allegedly mysterious circumstances in 2005. Todd Talby, 33, a local photographer, was reported missing from his home in Main Street, Fairwood, on 16 October. Heading the investigation, Det. Sgt. Ian Clay of Thames Valley Police told reporters 'We have no further information at this time'.